ESCAPING BLAKE

Mikayla Bowles

contents

CHAPTER 1

In the scientific world, the North side of a magnet is attracted to the South side of another magnet. When thrown together, a magnetic force is created between the two; a force so irrefutably strong that it cannot be stopped. In layman's terms, opposites attract.

This phrase not only applies in science, but in relationships. Considering relationships are generally based off common interests, its mind boggling to think that love interests can actually form between two completely and erratically different personalities. Following examples: Romeo and Juliet, Tony and Maria, and even Danny and Sandy.

How is this even possible? The less two people have in common, the less they will be able to relate to each other, thus resulting in a weak relationship. How is it that a preppy, goody two shoes and a reckless delinquent come together, despite their inability to relate and connect?

The answer: Love.

Although there is no love in the scientific world, it can be treated as an experiment, subjected to interfering variables and human error.

Love is the ultimate test. It's up to the lovers to correctly perform the procedure and magnetize themselves to the fullest degree, or else the experiment will blow up in their faces.

Living in a small town entailed going to a small high school. Going to a small high school implied that everyone knew everyone. Everyone knowing everyone meant endless drama, and no privacy.

Most residing families didn't move out of Oxford, Connecticut due to their love and contentment of the colonial town. The taxes were high, but the schools were strong. However, that meant that the majority of the student body had spent all of their education in the same public school system. Spending eleven years with the same group of people was exhausting.

By junior year, we had all had our embarrassing reputations exposed. Each person was defined not by his or her current achievements, but by their past mistakes. No one got a fresh start, and no one was safe from his or her previous horrors.

For example, in 9th grade, one of our varsity linebackers thought Arnold Schwarzenegger was the President of the United States, when he actually was only the Governor of California. While it was a stupid mistake, he was instantly labeled as an "unintelligent meat head." That reputation followed him for years, despite how many times he consecutively made the principal's honor roll.

As for me, I was never able to break out of the "preppy, smart, bound-for-Harvard League" shell. In 4th grade, I won the class spelling bee. In 7th grade, I had more books than friends. In 9th grade, I was elected class president.

But believe me, school wasn't my life.

Honestly, I'd rather be out with my friends or my boyfriend, Blake Salato, than studying at home. I'd rather wear comfortable converse and jeans, instead of my usual attire consisting of blazers and ballet flats.

Nevertheless, after years of struggling with who I was as a person, Blake "persuaded" me to accept my label as "Riley Jennings: Top of the Class; Candidate for Valedictorian; and Future Successful Business Woman." And so, I did – it was just easier that way.

Nevertheless, this past-lingering, secret-exposing, drama-causing, label-creating, pathetic excuse for a high school had me begging on my knees for the day I went to college. There I could be anyone I wanted to be, I could be the person I truly was - not the person people wanted me to be. I just needed to survive two more years of high school.

However, that was easier said than done.

Escaping the cold, late November wind, I walked into school through the main entrance doors expecting another regular day of school, no different than any other. But the moment I walked into the lobby, I knew things were different. Instead of the too-loud-to-think atmosphere, the open area was as quiet as a cemetery, as people talked in hushed tones.

As I passed the clusters of people, I tried catching tidbits of the most recent gossip. However, years of blasting my iPod too loudly prevented me to do so.

The whispers continued all the way to class. Even as I took my front seat in chemistry – my first period class – a group of people was huddled in the back, conversing in low voices. Fighting the desire to eavesdrop, I pulled out my notebook and started working on some calculus homework.

"You will not believe what I just heard," exclaimed my best friend, Lucy Wilde, as she smacked her backpack down next to me in excitement. "Apparently, we have a new juvenile delinquent transferring to our school. He's been kicked out of six schools, robbed two banks, and stabbed one guy."

That would explain all the hushed gossip.

"Are you sure? That sounds like a load of bull crap," I said, challenging the rumors.

"I don't know," she replied, shaking her head. "I guess we'll have to find out."

Lucy was fabulous. She was everything I wasn't: beautiful, confident, energetic, full of life. We had been inseparable for years and she was my rock. I never understood why someone like her chose to be friends with someone like me but I didn't dare question it.

As my best friend, Lucy was the one person I trusted most. She saw my good and bad side; she saw me at my best and worst. When I needed someone to dry my tears and ice my wounds, she was there for me.

Once the second bell rang, everyone put their rumor spreading agendas on halt. Our dry and utterly dimwitted teacher, Mr. Richards, pulled up a PowerPoint presentation and began to ramble on.

Lucky for us, somebody interrupted the droning presentation.

A dark, mysterious boy strutted in. A leather jacket, tight jeans, and black combat boots covered his tall, lean body. Dark, untamed hair framed his strong-featured face. Sure, he was good-looking, but Blake's face flashed through my mind, warning me to keep my distance.

"Is this Chemistry with Richards?" The deep-voiced boy asked, checking the schedule in his hand.

"Right it is," Mr. Richards exclaimed enthusiastically. His voice was shriller than it had been all period. "Take a seat, Mister . . ."

"Marks," the husky voice answered. "Dean Marks."

All eyes were on Dean Marks as he gracefully slid into the empty chair at the end of the front row. Casually, he took his leather jacket off, hung it on the back of his chair, and rolled up his flannel sleeves, exposing tattooed forearms.

Despite the distraction, Mr. Richards began teaching again. With all my willpower, I continued to follow the presentation slides and take detailed notes. As most of the girls fawned over Dean, most of the boys fumed with jealousy, leaving me to be one of the few students to actually pay attention.

Class ended, but the usual barricade to the door did not exist today. Many of the girls lingered around, hoping to snag a moment of conversation with the new kid. Only the school slut, Penelope Ruth, was bold enough to approach him and ask if he needed directions.

"Yeah," he nodded, as he slipped out his schedule. "Where is the English department?"

"Oh, I can show you," she offered, smacking her gum and twisting a lock of fiery red hair.

"Uh actually." His eyes darted around the room. "I'm all set, thanks," he finally replied, obviously not fooled by her seductive tricks.

After he left, the crowd of girls fled after him, leaving me alone to ask Mr. Richards my question on what we had just learned about Planck's theory. Although I had a free period, I knew I had to hurry because Blake would be waiting for me.

Once I understood the concept, I sloppily packed my bag and ran down the stairwell, through the hallways, across the outside crosswalk and into the junior parking lot. Despite my rushing efforts, I was not fast enough.

Leaning against the side of his pickup truck, Blake was already waiting. He had parked in the last row of the parking lot, next to the shivering trees naked from winter's brutality. His blue eyes were filled with rage as his lips were curled into a bitter scowl. Chills ran up through my back as I approached him.

The parking lot was empty for the most part. Almost everyone had class, and those who had free periods like us usually went to the library rather than venturing out into the cold. It was just Blake and I as far as the eye could see.

"Where were you?" He asked, forcing a calm voice.

I tried to catch my breath and looked down at my black leather wrist watch. I was more than 15 minutes late. In Blake's world, 15 minutes might as well have been 15 hours.

"I was just asking my teacher a question," I replied, meekly. My knees weakened as my back arched, but I forced myself to stand tall.

"Oh really?" He tested, his voice growing harsher. The November wind was blowing through his blond hair, making him look even more menacing.

"Yeah, we just learned about Planck's theory and I was just clearing some confusion up," I explained, hoping he would understand.

But deep down, I knew better than that. It didn't matter if he understood or believe me, even when it was the honest to God truth. If he was upset about something, anything . . . it was my automatically fault. That's just the way it was with him.

As he yanked on my ponytail with great force, Blake spat, "You better not be lying to me."

I winced through the pain but tried my best to steady my voice. "I'm not, I swear! I would never lie to you!"

With all of his football-trained strength, he pushed me onto the cold pavement. "You know, you're full of shit. A smart girl like you doesn't need extra help, you're too good for that."

On my knees, shaking from the cold, I snapped inside. "I'm not the smart girl that everyone thinks I am! You're the one who wants me to be like this!"

He slapped me across the face. "How dare you talk back to me? Yeah, I do want you like this, because that's all your good for. It's all you have going for you, because let's face it; you're nothing special." He paused to catch his breath and kicked the back bumper of somebody else's car. "God, I can't even look at you."

Leaving me on the ground, sobbing, Blake turned on his heel, got in his truck and slammed the door shut. With quick acceleration, the car screamed as he sped off.

The thing about an abusive relationship is you can't walk away. Most people don't get that. The threats, the fear; it all prevents you from saying no and ending it all once and for good. You're afraid of what the person will do to you if you reject them. When you've been beaten down enough times, you lose all the strength you once had. You become the person that your abuser wants you to be.

Fear consumes you, both physically and mentally, and you lose yourself. Eventually, you become nothing; not a person, not a human being, just a crying voice that gets lost in the wind.

By this point in our relationship, I couldn't hide, because he would find me. A few months ago, I tried ending things with Blake after one of his bloodiest beatings. That didn't work out too well. Blake came to my house after I got back from the hospital, apologized, and said he never hurt me again. Of course, that turned out to be just another lie. After that, I never tried ending it again, because I knew what he was capable of . . . ending my life.

CHAPTER 2

As pathetic as it was, the bitter, numbing, winter air was actually more pleasant than Blake. Or should I say . . . the new Blake.

Blake wasn't always this way. In the beginning of our relationship, I was the luckiest girl in the world. Blake was attractive, charming, sensitive, and not to mention quarterback for the varsity football team. When we first started dating, he treated me like a princess. Blake would give me the kindest compliments, take me to the nicest restaurants, and take care of me when I was afraid, stressed, or worried.

About a month into our relationship, I spent every free moment with Blake and not with my friends. And when I started allocating my time a bit better, he began asking constant questions; about where I was, what I was doing or who I was doing whatever it was with. If I chose my friends over him, he would throw a hissy fit. When he saw me talking to other guys, jealousy would consume him. Lucy warned me and tried to tell me that these were bad signs, but I didn't believe her. I was so young and naïve back then; I truly thought it was his way of showing he deeply cared about me.

I should have listened to her.

Naturally, we started fighting, but Blake would always manage to turn the tables and blame me. Blake felt the need to control my life: whom I hung out with, how I presented myself, what I was labeled as. Before I knew it, my life had flipped 180 degrees. Eventually, his jealousy became anger. His meaningless threats turned into punches. And my love for him turned into disgusted hate.

As I rested on the cold pavement, my sobs degraded to whimpers. I wasn't sure how much time I had wasted, but at this mental state, I was in no hurry to go anywhere. Even after I regained some composure, I remained in the fetal position on the ground just contemplating the world. I couldn't tell if this was rock bottom; and if it was, would I ever go up? For some reason, in the pit of my stomach that filled me up with the nausea of a sailor, I knew that the worst had yet to come.

I wasn't too worried about anyone seeing me because nobody wandered around the parking lot in the middle of the period - if anyone did decide to be bold and endure the cold weather, they left in the beginning and returned at the end.

But there was one person who hadn't conformed to the daily routines of Oxford High School yet.

"Are you okay?" A recently familiar voice asked. Startled and yet still exhausted, I rolled over on my side. When I saw those dark wash jeans tucked into leather combat boots, I instantly sat up.

"Yeah," I mumbled, embarrassed. "I . . . uh . . . fell . . . on some ice, I think."

"You fell?" Dean repeated, suspiciously. "How long have you been there?"

"I don't know, not long," I shrugged. "I lost track of time."

"You must have hit your head pretty hard," he muttered. He squatted down next to me. "You're bleeding."

After being beaten so many times, I was no longer able to judge the amount of damage done. Each slap, punch, push felt the same – a universal level of pain, hate, shock, and betrayal.

Pulling a handkerchief from his pocket, Dean reached out and dabbed the side of my forehead. I watched as the white linen cloth became speckled with drops of red blood. The cursive initials BK stitched into the handkerchief in navy blue thread caught my attention, but I didn't think to ask about it.

"Thanks," I muttered, quietly. Dean handed me the handkerchief so I could continue putting pressure on my cut.

"No problem. Just try to be more careful, okay? I'm Dean by the way," he said, still crouching down next to me.

"Oh yeah, I think you're in my chemistry class," I replied. "I'm Riley. Do you have a free period right now or something?"

"No, it's just my job to stay around here and make sure nobody is lying on the ground, helplessly," Dean teased, mocking my suspicious behavior. "But really, I just couldn't find my classroom, so I decided to give up and skip."

"Oh . . ." I replied, rubbing my throbbing temple. "Makes sense, I guess."

If I wasn't so utterly upset about Blake, I might have actually had an aneurysm because I was actually talking to the infamous new kid. But I couldn't process that this was real life, and so to me, Dean appeared to be just the same as anyone else. Generally, after a violent fight with Blake, I was spacey and incoherent for a bit, unable to identify reality from fantasy. After a while, my whole life started to feel like one hazy dream, anyway.

"Well, if I showed up within the next five minutes, I could just use the excuse that I got lost on my first day," Dean hinted, with a playful tone. "I've got American Literature with Hollins."

Her classroom was right across from my AP Language room. With a sigh, I said, "I'll take you there. I should probably head in that direction anyway, since the nurse's office is in the next hallway over."

Dean offered me a hand, and without skipping a beat, I grabbed it. I didn't even think about the hot, tingling sensation that traveled up my arm from touching his rough, calloused skin. In that moment, I was just thankful for the helping hand, and that was the sad truth.

Leaving the cold, we walked slowly towards the East Wing of the campus. Dean was polite enough not to speed ahead, acknowledging that I needed a few minutes to regain my balance and coordination. When we approached the nurse's office first, Dean told me he could figure out the rest of the way to his class.

"Are you sure? Just keep walking straight, take a right and you'll be there," I directed. Remembering the bloody handkerchief, I extended it out in front of me, and said, "Here. Thanks . . . sorry I ruined it."

"Keep it," he replied, probably disgusted by sight of my dark, crusty blood. "I have more at home."

"Thanks," I muttered, embarrassed at myself. "Good luck with finding everything."

"Good luck with not falling to your death," he joked, before walking away. Halfway down the hallway, he called, "See you around."

I watched his rear side as he sauntered away, using the hallway as his catwalk. Coming back into my regular state of mind, I was beginning to process the sweet but brief interaction we just had. Glancing down at Dean's bloody handkerchief, I felt myself smiling at the delicately sewn mysterious initials as my fingers traced along.

You know, despite all of the rumors going around, he didn't seem half bad. Indeed he had a rough exterior, but based off his kindness towards a complete stranger, I couldn't imagine he would be the type to stab someone?

I shook him away from my mind before I began to overthink anything. Besides, I had bigger things to worry about than the new kid offering a helping hand to someone in need.

Before entering the nurse's office, I debated if I should keep the handkerchief or not. If I kept it, I was risking the chance of Blake seeing it. But why should I throw out a perfectly good handkerchief? I decided that I would wash it, get all the blood stains out, and somehow give it back to Dean. There, problem solved.

Slipping the bloody handkerchief into the front pocket of my backpack, I entered the office. The nurse cleaned my cut with some antibacterial solution and strategically placed the band-aid so that my hair covered it.

My next few classes flowed normally. The throbbing pain Blake had inflicted had disappeared, the handkerchief was out of my sight, and neither of them were in any of my classes. Class served as a useful distraction, and before I knew it, today didn't seem to be any different than any other day.

By the time the lunch period rolled around, that horrible feeling of guilt and agony was in the pit of my stomach again. But I was used to it and did my best to ignore. Through the hustle and bustle of ravenous kids all trying to feed, I managed to find Lucy. Of course, I kept my mouth shut about the earlier events. There was no need to worry her. After we filled our trays with mediocre cafeteria slop, we joined the rest of our friends at our usual lunch table. No surprise that the table's main conversation was about Dean.

Uncomfortably, I felt the need to tune out of the conversation. There was no reason for me to participate in the gossip, especially when I wasn't entirely sure if I agreed with it.

Instead, I scanned the football table for Blake's face. His piercing blue eyes met mine, which sent a wave of fear through my body. Finally, he broke the eye connection, and looked downward. A few moments later, I felt my phone buzz:

From: Blake

Sorry about earlier...u know I love u right?

Knowing Blake was watching me for my reaction, I stopped myself from rolling my eyes at his pathetic, insincere apology. Repeatedly, this was his way of justifying his actions.

When you're really sorry, you learn from their mistakes and vow never to do it again. When you love someone, you never want to harm them in any way. Neither of these applied to Blake, which proved the illegitimacy of what he just said. Knowing I had to please him, I replied:

To: Blake

Its ok, love u 2

I watched as a seemingly genuine smirk arose on his face.

From the outside, a guy can seem perfect; in looks, in reputation, in personality. From the outside, a girl can seem happily content with her studious life and her perfect boyfriend. From the outside, a relationship can seem flawless and problem-free.

It's not until you step inside, peel off the outer layer, turn the next page, that you see the other side of the story. If I have learned one thing from this detrimental relationship, it's that nothing is as it seems. Everything and everyone has another side, another layer, another face, and another story.

CHAPTER 3

Every day, Blake was my ride home, no matter what series of unfortunate events may have occurred earlier. His commitment to driving me home was the only good-natured deed he performed on a regular basis.

As soon as the last bell rings, the halls, the lobby, and the parking lots are massacred and stampeded by rowdy teenagers, desperate to escape the school. Within five minutes, the school is deserted in the dead of silence. This rapid transition of atmosphere always marveled me. Before I started dating Blake, I would sit on a blue metal bench pushed against the side of the lobby, and observe as the people passed by, until the place was empty.

I savored that vacant period so much because it was the only time in school that I could actually be myself. Mr. Pewter, the music conductor, left his room unlocked everyday so people could sign out an instrument, and borrow it for the afternoon. Of course, due to every students desire to leave immediately, the instrumental loaning system was barely used. Except, by me.

When the school was deserted, I would head over to the G-Wing and sign out the acoustic guitar. Since discovering an obsession with female rocker, Joan Jett, my lust to learn the guitar was overwhelming. Joan Jett was everything I wanted to be, but couldn't. She was edgy, fierce, stylish and mentally strong. She didn't care what people thought of her, and she definitely did not let anyone mess with her. Playing guitar gave me a small taste of her inner strength. So every day during my alone time, I would teach myself a little bit.

I was actually starting to get pretty good, but once Blake came into my life, my personal guitar lessons came to an end. It was what I missed and needed most; I could have used a tiny bit of Joan's "don't fuck with me" attitude to finally stand up to Blake.

Nowadays, like everyone else, I hustled with the pack out of the school. As I walked towards Blake's black pickup truck, I noticed that he wasn't there yet. Of course, it was okay to keep me waiting, but it wasn't okay to keep him waiting.

So I leaned against the side of his car, tapped my foot, and anticipated his arrival. Eventually, Blake departed from his football pack and greeted me. As he pulled me into a hug, my body unintentionally flinched — even the slightest, kindest touch from him psychologically frightened me.

I resembled the rescue dog my aunt had when I was a kid. Tiger, retrieved from the Bahamas, was a mix breed who had been physically abused by her former owner. When anyone tried to pet her, she would immediately wince, in response to her horrific memories. The physical wounds may fade, but the emotional scars linger forever.

"Hey babe," Blake greeted, taking my face in his hands and kissing me.

"Hi," I replied, trying my hardest to seem pleased by the affection. Bu deep down, I knew that a tender kiss doesn't heal a bloody bruise.

The loud growl of a motorbike broke our embrace. Swiveling our heads around, we saw a dark figure maneuvering a navy blue BMW model. Although the rider was wearing a dark tinted helmet that covered their face, I knew exactly who it was. Dean, who was casually passing by, revved his engine up again, startling Blake even more.

"Asshole," Blake muttered, walking around the side of the car and climbing into the driver's seat. Takes one to know one.

Once I was strapped into the passenger seat, Blake said, "We just have a make a stop at the station first."

Peter Salato, Blake's father, held the chief position at Oxford State Police Force for over fifteen years. Although he was impeccable at his job, his rank prevented me from turning Blake in for his domestic violence and assaults. Peter Salato was no Barty Crouch, Sr. If I ever tried to call the cops on Blake, I'm pretty sure the dispatcher would laugh in my face.

As regulars, Blake and I casually strolled through the department. With humble greetings, we passed along the cubicles until we arrived at Peter's office. The glass-paneled door was ajar, so we stepped inside.

Reclining in his large leather chair, Officer Peter was chatting away on the phone, feet elevated onto his desk. When he saw us enter, he signaled us to sit down.

Peter was a pudgy man, with a plump, round face and slick, grey hair. His clothes never fit, sometimes too large, sometimes too small. He had blue piercing eyes, just like Blake. Other than eyes, they shared the same belief in "tough love." Like father like son.

"Okay . . . yeah I'm just basing off the report . . . no, just one witness . . . uh huh . . . okay, will do." Officer Peter hung the phone up, and then turned his attention to us. "How was school?"

"Same as usual," Blake replied. I shrugged, restraining from verbal agreement with Blake's response.

"Did you get the school record?" Officer Peter leaned forward, his voice low and secretive.

"Right here," Blake answered, pulling a school folder out of his backpack. My eyebrows crinkled in suspicion.

"Excellent," Peter smugly grinned, opening it up. His eyes glazed over my confused expression, but he chose to ignore it. I fought the bad feeling I got from this because it was none of my business.

"See you at home," Blake said, rising from his seat. He formally shook his father's hand, and exited.

"Bye Mr. Salato," I said, as if it actually mattered. After all, I was practically invisible to their family.

According to Mrs. Salato, because I didn't come from a rich, upper class family like she did, I wasn't good enough. It didn't matter that my family chose to live a modest life rather than conspicuous consumption, it didn't matter that I was destined for a well-endorsed career that would lead to my utter success, and it didn't matter that her husband came from a similar family upbringing – in her eyes, I would never be good enough.

Back in the car, Blake put on some revolting new age techno that gave me a migraine. I rested my face against the cool car window, hoping it would soothe the shooting pains.

Blake placed a hand on my thigh. "You okay?"

Like you actually care, I almost replied. But I couldn't bring myself to say the words, I never could. Holding my tongue was like swallowing acid; the words burned as they traveled back down in my throat. I've begged myself for the courage to stand up to him, bitch him out, speak my mind. But it was always the fear that held me back and cut me down.

After silently nodding, I resumed my head resting position. After pulling my hood up and closing my eyes, I tried to block out the robotic notes. Instead, I tried imagining Joan Jett's "Love Is Pain" as I fingered the chords in the air.

"Hey," Blake snapped, violently shoving my shoulder, interrupting my musical haven. "I asked you a question. Answer it."

Startled, I removed my hood and scowled. "What did you ask? I wasn't paying attention."

"I asked . . . do you know about the new kid?"

My heart dropped, my stomach twisted into pretzels, and my hands suddenly became sweaty. Was this a trick?

"Uh . . . yeah . . . he's um in my chemistry class," I stuttered, tripping over my words. Luckily, Blake didn't seem to notice.

"That bitch-ass punk is up to no good," Blake spat. "I'm telling you, he's trouble."

I didn't feel like replying to his remark. This "new-kid" obsession was starting to really bug me. Choosing not to continue the subject, the remainder of the car ride was silent. Blake didn't seem to mind; as long as his crappy, artificial music was playing, he was satisfied.

We finally pulled up to my modest two-story house estate. Respectively, we had one acre of land, a 2-car garage, and more than sufficient room space for a household of four. Although we weren't as wealthy as the surplus Salatos, we were pretty well off.

With a quick, unfavorable cheek peck, I jumped out of the pickup truck, grabbed the mail, and entered through the front door. My cocker spaniel, Athena, eagerly greeted me, dowsing my hand with saliva as her tail wagged rapidly.

Because both of my parents worked, I had the house to myself. My younger brother didn't get out of middle school until 3:15, which left me with a solid twenty minutes to myself. Before our relationship turned into what it is now, Blake and I would use this time to get intimate. These days, I spent my time indulging into my journal.

Inside a small red leather journal held every single thought of mine. Full of lists, song lyrics, doodles, and confessions, that book held my life. Writing my thoughts, clearing my head, helped me push through every tough, discouraging day. Without it, I would be a wreck; the tragedy and madness would pry into my mind, driving me into either insanity or depression. I decided today's entry would be a poem themed record.

Good or bad . . .

Right or wrong . . .

Suffering and sad . .

Or surviving strong . . .

The decision lies within our core

The rejected washes upon the shore

Are we defined by our choice of side?

Stuck with our pick for life, an eternal tie?

Indecisive, neutral, and free I'd rather be.

I closed my journal, tied it with a ribbon, and slipped it between my mattress, where it would remain hidden from the world until tomorrow.

CHAPTER 4

"Riley?" My mother's voice echoed from the kitchen to my bedroom. "Could you set the table?"

Sighing, I put down my Latin textbook and accepted my mother's request. The smell of rosemary chicken, au gratin potatoes, and steamed broccoli filled every open room of the house. My little brother, Charlie, was sprawled out on the living room couch, reading his newest comic book. My father was lounging in his big leather chair on the opposite side of the room, reading today's issue of the New York Times. My mother, still dressed in her pencil skirt suit, was diligently cooking in the kitchen. Wisps of hair had fallen out of her earlier perfect work bun, framing her make-up faded face.

Collecting all of the necessary dining utensils, I began to set the table for four people.

"Thanks, honey," Mom said, mashing up the potatoes. "How was your day?"

"Fine," I replied. A neutral, one-word answer was better than explaining my negatively eventful day.

Pouring myself a glass of iced tea, I took my seat the dining table. My mother plopped the food down in the center of the table and called for the boys to join us.

With my plate loaded, I indulged into my mother's superb meal. Quietly eating, I tuned out of my parent's discussion about their workdays. Charlie was doing the same, except he was sneaking pieces of broccoli and chicken under the table for Athena.

"Riley!" My mother exclaimed. "What the hell happened to you?" A sliver of my head bandage must have peaked out from under my hair because she was pushing back my hairline to get a better examination of my concealed wound.

"I fell on some ice," I murmured, repeating the same lie I gave Dean. I snuck a glance at my father, who gave me a knowledgeable stare.

Dad knows about Blake. At first, he was smitten by Blake's charm and appeal, in the same way I was. But he knew the truth as soon as I did. The first beating left me with a severe black eye. When my father asked about it, I said some girl elbowed me in P.E during volleyball. He saw right through me. After all, as a criminal case lawyer, that's his job - uncovering the truth behind a story. He's doing his best to help, but he's seen a lot of court cases with similar situations, and the end results are never pretty . . . It's hard for him, knowing what's at stake, knowing what could possibly happen to his daughter.

I know sometimes he wishes he could be a normal, impulsive father who calls the police or beats the crap out of Blake, but he's different. He's seen too much to know the dire consequences of acting irrationally. He's the one that has stressed to me that we need to handle this situation delicately and strategically because he's seen it all. After studying dozens of cases where the abuser ends up either raping or killing their victim after filing for a restraining order, he knows the precautions he has to take. It doesn't help that Blake exhibits the same bi-polar, sociopathic behavior as the ones that commit murder: the obsession, the irrational aggression, the manipulation, the denial and disillusion of reality. I trust in my father's wisdom and guidance on the matter and I'm honestly grateful that he's not reacting like people think a father should. I know that sounds twisted, but for me, it's a matter of life or death.

Dad and I have been working together for quite some time, devising a plan of how to take Blake down. Maybe we're not taking the conventional route, but this isn't a conventional case. Like every abuse situation, it's not as cut and dry as some may think. And with the forces we have working against us, it only makes things ten times harder. In order for this to override Chief Salato's jurisdiction, it has to be taken to court at the federal level. And to that, we need a strong enough case. Like Rome, a winning case isn't built in one day. It takes time, evidence, witnesses and even some blood and tears. But we were getting close . . . very close. One day soon, justice would be served.

Mom, on the other hand, is blissfully unaware. When it comes to conflicting, serious situations, my mother freaks out. And that's an understatement. She can't handle any sort of decision-making or uncomfortable pressure, so when she faces a conflict of great gravity, she cracks; breaks downs and falls into a dark, gloomy period for a few weeks. It's easier for all of us to keep her out of the loop.

As for Charlie. . . Dad says it's too early to tell him, especially because he currently idolizes Blake. We're waiting till we both think he is ready

Dad, as always, went along with it. "Our daughter, the graceful swan."

"Yeah, I was born to be a ballerina . . ."

"Riley, I wish you would be more careful," my mother sternly said.

"I'll try," I replied, through gritted teeth.

After we finished our meal, we all cleared our plates and headed into our separate ways - my brother to the television, my mother to her soothing bath, my father to his study, and I back to my homework.

When I finished, I took a long leisurely shower. Other than my shampoo stinging my open cut, the hot shower was incredibly relaxing. After I dried off, I got ready for bed. Although it was only 9, I was exhausted from the long, busy day. Besides, I would probably spend an hour or so reading. Curled up under my covers, I was enjoying in the pages of Gone With The Wind, when there was a knock at my door.

"Come in," I called, dog-earring the page.

My father entered and took a seat on the edge of my bed. He also ready for bed, in his flannel pajamas and moccasin slippers. Wearing his out-dated, oversized, 1980's style glasses, I assumed he had already taken his contacts out for the night.

"Good book," he patted the cover of my book, "even better movie."

"But the movie leaves out so many important details," I replied.

My father removed his glasses and rubbed his eyes. "Don't you ever just want to be a normal teenage girl?"

"Normal is overrated. Besides, I think it's a little too late for that anyway."

"It's never too late for anything," Dad said. "So you want to tell me what really happened today?"

I shrugged. "I stayed after class to ask my teacher something, Blake flipped out because I was late meeting him, he accused me of lying, he drove off, and then he worked up some lame apology."

"The usual. What about the car ride home?"

"Now that you mention it . . . there was something else. Blake handed his father a school record folder . . . I'm assuming he stole it or something because the school doesn't regularly hand out confidential informational documents to students."

My father crinkled his eyebrows but didn't say anything in response, which was a good sign.

"Well goodnight," he uttered, kissing my cheek.

"Don't keep yourself up all night," I replied, opening my book and flipping to the dog-eared page.

"No promises," he called, before closing the bedroom door behind him.

My alarm went off, disrupting both my REM cycle and my dream. I don't remember what it was about, but I was enjoying it. My book, which I don't recall putting down, was now on the floor.

After my morning routine - shower, dress, and bagel - I pulled on my peacoat and waited at the bus stop. I hated taking the bus, but I had no choice. Blake always had morning football practice, my parents left for work around 6:30-7, and I didn't have my license yet.

After the monotonous bus ride, I walked into school, unsure of what the day held. While most days were fairly repetitive, like a broken record stuck on the same track, occasionally the unexpected happened. Yesterday was a perfect example.

As my morning classes droned on, I accepted the fact that today was not going to be a special occasion. Believe or not, that was usually a good thing. Even Chemistry, with the unquestionably gorgeous Dean Marks, was rather uneventful.

Despite his head turning looks and infamous reputation, Dean practically blended into my science class. He sat quietly at the end of the row of desks; never asked questions, never gave answers, and never spoke to anyone. Clearly, he was the type to keep to himself and I kind of admired that. Regardless of the budding interaction, we had yesterday, all I got was a modest, low-key wave from him when he walked into class. Being the new kid, he probably felt uncomfortable in his new, populated surrounding.

My afternoon classes were turning out to be just as tedious as my morning classes when an announcement was made over the school's intercom.

"Riley Jennings, please report to the guidance office immediately."

All eyes were on me, as I sheepishly left my AP US History classroom. Walking down the hall, I wondered what my guidance counselor needed me for. Generally, meetings were scheduled with students during free periods, so being called out of class was unusual.

Reaching the guidance office, I passed the secretary's desk and headed straight for my guidance counselor's room. After one knock on the ajar door, she invited me in.

Mrs. Delgado was a petite, fragile, and stern elderly woman. Every day, she looked the exactly same; hair pulled back in a ridiculously scalping chignon, frumpy pantsuit, and crimson red lipstick that traveled from her lips to her teeth.

"Glad you could make it," Mrs. Delgado greeted. Typical response for her. Other guidance counselors might have said something like, "sorry to pull you out of class on such short notice." But not for Mrs. Delgado.

"I don't know if you've heard, but we have a new student in our school," she started. Letting out a sigh, I nodded. The new kid hype was spreading larger and lasting longer than I predicted.

"He's in my Chemistry class."

"I noticed that when I was looking over both of your class schedules," she replied, lacing her long bony fingers together. "You see, Dean's what I like to call 'unapplied intelligence.'" Separating her hands, she made air quotes. "For new transfers, we require an IQ test. Dean scored relatively high, above average than most, which means he's got the potential. However, Dean doesn't seem like the type of person who is willing to apply himself to his work, preventing him from getting the grades he deserves. Seeing as this is his fifth consecutive high school, I want to inspire a change in him. I don't want to see him flunk out or get expelled again like he did in his previous schools. I have a great deal of faith in him. He seems to be a bit misguided with his priorities, and I'm hoping you can help him on the right path."

"Me?" I heard a faint hint of surprise and intimidation in my voice. "I don't know if that's such a good idea . . ."

"Why not? You're utterly brilliant, top of the class, headed for greatness. If anyone can help him, it's you," she replied, obviously trying to sell me the idea. "Plus, it'll look great for college. It'll give your applications some extra spice."

Of course, she pulled out the college card. She knew that my deepest desire was to get into that perfect college and leave this stupid town behind. That's why she was so good at her job; she knew everything about her students.

"I don't know . . ." I averted my gaze to the floor.

"What's holding you back?" Her voice was filled with concern.

She asked a question that I couldn't answer. My reply was imprisoned in the core of my body, and I knew better than to unlock it.

"I don't think I have time," I lied.

"I can assure you that won't be an issue," she said. "All I need you to do is just tutor him once or twice a week. Help him with organizing his work, answer his questions when he doesn't understand the material, show him that doing the work pays off. It wouldn't have to be a full-time commitment, just for a while until he's ready to be on his own. I can't help but wonder if the real problem has been with the other schools. Perhaps they didn't offer enough for him to succeed, and his discouragement caused him to fall into this workless habit."

When she put it that way, it didn't sound so bad. It actually sounded kind of morally upholding, like helping a lost soul find it's way. I pondered for a bit, weighing out the Pros and Cons.

"Looks good for college, did you say?"

"Indeed. Universities love to see leadership, generosity, Peer-to-Peer tutoring," she informed, with a convincing smile.

Maybe I just wouldn't tell Blake about it. Not necessarily lie, just hide the truth. After all, he didn't own me, he wasn't my husband. I didn't know every detail of his life, so why should he know every detail of mine?

"Okay," I replied, taking a deep breath. "I'll do it."

CHAPTER 5

"Wonderful!" Mrs. Delgado clapped her hands together. "Think you could start today?"

"I guess," I muttered, having no legitimate reason to say no.

"Great, I'll let Dean know right away," she said, scribbling onto a neon green Post-It. "You guys will meet after school in the library. You're free to go."

I nodded, bid my farewell, and headed back to class. Walking through the deserted hallways, I contemplated the disaster I had just gotten myself into. Tutoring Dean was another lie to be told, another secret to be hidden, and another burden on my plate. If word got out, I was screwed.

And yet, I was almost excited for this opportunity. It felt wrong, but it felt right. In my mind, I was spiting, betraying, and disregarding Blake. Similar to playing the guitar, it gave me a sense of power and rebellion; all strength I would later need.

By the time I got back, the class was practically over. I quickly jotted down the remainder of notes on the board and then packed up my backpack. When the bell rang, I hurried down to the lobby, hoping to catch Blake before he headed for the parking lot.

Searching through the sea of people, I found him standing in a big huddle with his football friends. When the cheerleaders began to break into the circle, I did the same.

"Hey baby," he greeted, kissing my cheek. I choked back a noise of disgust. Before lowering his voice, he scanned the faces of his friends to make sure they weren't watching. "You want to tell me what that announcement was about?"

The thing I hated most about our relationship was the lack of privacy. It wasn't the violence or the limitations or the hurtful words - it was the fact that he needed to know every bit of information about my life.

"Just some college stuff," I lied. "Look, I have to stay after school so you don't need to drive me home."

Blake glared at me through skeptical eyes. "Oh okay. And what are you staying after school for?"

"Just a thing," I replied with a shrug. At least I didn't lie that time, I just avoided the truth.

"What kind of thing?" Blake asked again, his cheeks turning a shade of crimson.

"Nothing, don't worry about it," I answered, brushing him off. Already, the strength was building inside of me.

Blake's eyes filled with fire, his jaw clenched in fury, his breathing pattern grew heavier. "You better tell me, or else -"

"You'll what?" I cut him off. "Hit me? No, you won't. Not in front of everyone."

He wanted to hurt me, he wanted to cause me pain, he wanted me to cry until I learned my lesson, he wanted me to beg for mercy and apologize. But he knew better than to cause that kind of scene in such a public place.

Blake took a step closer to me and whispered, "You may have gotten away with this bullshit of yours this time, but I don't forget anything."

After he stormed out the front doors, I cowered into a corner and broke into uncontrollable shivers. The victory and the fear were too opposite for my emotions to handle at the same time. I was both fearless and fearful, triumphant and defeated, invincible and vulnerable. I had won this quarrel, but who knew if I would win the next one.

I lifted my shaking arm and checked my wristwatch. Knowing that Dean was waiting for me, I took a few breaths and tried to calm myself down. When I was ready, I got up, brushed the dust from my skirt and walked towards the library.

Once I was there, I spotted Dean, sitting at one of the wooden, square tables in the back. His head was bent over, his hands were in his lap, and his feet were elevated on the table. I slowly approached him, trying not to startle or disturb him too much.

"Well, would you look at this," he said, once he saw me. "The one girl I know at this school just happens to be my tutor."

"Just a coincidence."

Putting on my best act, I tried to seem as normal as possible. He had already seen me once in utter despair; a second time would peak his curiosity, which was the last thing I needed.

"How's that cut doing?" My fingers lightly pressed against the area on my head.

"Better." Reminded of his kind gesture, I made a mental note to wash the handkerchief before the next tutoring session. "So, where should we begin?"

"I don't know, you tell me," he replied, lacing his hands behind his head. His biceps flexed through his tight, long sleeved shirt.

"Why don't we start with your favorite subject?"

"Don't have one," Dean answered, with a modest smirk.

"Come on, there's got to be something you like," I replied.

"Well, I like to read," Dean admitted. "But that doesn't mean I like English."

"That's a start. What are you reading in class right now?"

Dean pulled a paper-back book out of his bag, slid it across the table, and raised a dark eyebrow at me - To Kill a Mocking Bird.

"Oh, this is one of my favorites!" I exclaimed, scrounging up a bit of enthusiasm.

"That makes one of us," Dean muttered, rolling his eyes.

I took his attitude as a bit of a challenge. "Okay then, Mr. Smart-Ass, what's your favorite book?"

"Doesn't matter."

"If you don't tell me, I won't be able to help you," I said, growing more serious by the minute.

"I didn't ask for your help. I didn't ask the school for any help quite frankly," Dean snapped. His dark eyes didn't match his bold words.

"Then why are you here? Why did you show up? If you don't want to change your ways, if you don't want to work, then leave. Nobody's stopping you."

Dean's eyes met mine, burning into my core. But unlike Blake, I wasn't afraid or intimidated by Dean. Here, I was an equal, playing on the same field level. I keep the eye connection, waiting for him to stand up and leave. But he didn't.

Instead, he silently pulled out a folder and reached across the table for his book. He ran his fingers through his dark, untamed hair and cracked open the novel.

After a few turned pages, he said, "Are you just going to sit there and watch? Or are you going to help me?"

Together, we spent the hour diligently working. Mrs. Delgado was right; Dean was incredibly smart. His analysis of the text was mind blowing, his insight was brilliant. The only thing that was preventing him from being in the high ranks was his lack of motivation. I couldn't help him with that; determination was something he had to do on his own.

"If you don't mind me asking," Dean asked, still writing in his notebook. "Why are you in standard Chemistry?"

I shrugged. "I like science but I've just never been really good at it. Why do you ask?"

"At least you admit you have flaws. I don't know, I was just curious because it seems like every other class you take is an honors course," Dean said, looking up from his work. "How do you do it?"

"Hard work? I don't know, sometimes it feels like a lot, but I've just gotten use to it over the years."

"So I'm guessing you want to go to Yale or Harvard, something like that."

"Not really," I replied. Dean raised his eyebrows in mild shock. "I'm working hard now, but that doesn't mean I want to work even harder in college. I'm going to go to a good school . . . the right school for me, and do want I want to do. Maybe that means ivy league and maybe not."

"Sure it does! I heard you're the smartest girl in school," Dean said.

"That's what everyone thinks, and I'm sick of it. I'm not as smart as I pretend to be," I said, feeling resentment towards the reputation I was forced to accept.

"Your grades beg to differ," Dean muttered, looking back down at his notes.

"It's not about the grades anymore. After college, grades don't matter. They don't define you. Real intelligence is important. Dean, you're just as smart as me, probably even more so. You've got smarts that will help you succeed the real world. As for me, I only know how to do well on a test which means I'm practically screwed once we graduate. I'm no smarter than anyone else," I said, looking down as well so he wouldn't see the tears that had formed in the corner of my eyes.

"Riley," he said, reaching over the table and grabbed my hand. His hand was rough and warm around mine. "Look at me." Hesitantly, I lifted my eyes, knowing he could see my glassy eyes. "You're brilliant, book and street wise. Don't ever let someone tell you differently. We all have our strengths and weaknesses, but that only leaves room for improvement."

I held onto his hand for a little bit longer, before skillfully slipping out of his grasp. Dean's small, comforting gesture filled me with more affection than Blake ever did in our months of serious dating.

Wiping my watery eyes, I checked my watch. "Looks like our session is practically over."

"Awesome," Dean replied, throwing on his leather jacket. "Let me give you a ride home. It's the least I can do after all your help."

Originally, I planned on calling my mother to pick me up. But his offer was too good to resist, so I accepted. We left the library and started walking towards the G-Wing.

"Where are we going?"

"I just have to make a stop at the music room," Dean answered.

My heart stopped beating for a moment or two. For the first time in months, I would enter my sanctuary. When we got there, the same stingy, yet comforting smell filled my nostrils. Everything looked the same, not a thing out of place. While Dean searched the room for something in particular, I wandered to the acoustic guitar, locked up in its dusty case. My fingers ran over the smooth, black surface, longing to open it.

"Found it," Dean said, holding up wooden drumsticks. Startled, I jumped away from the guitar. Dean walked over to me and said, "Do you play?"

"Kind of . . ."

"Well then, let me hear," he said, sitting in a plastic blue chair, looking up at me with eager eyes.

"I can't. I haven't played in a really long time."

"So what? It's like riding a bicycle, right? You never forget."

In a desperate attempt, I tried changing the subject. "Do you play the drums?"

Unfortunately, he saw right through me. "Yes, yes I do. But I'm not standing in the spotlight right now . . . you are."

Knowing I wasn't getting out of this, I unlocked the silver clasps and removed the guitar from its case. After the strings were tuned I said, "You were warned."

"Fair enough," Dean said, raising his hands up. "Go on, play!"

Arranging my fingers into a D Major chord, I strummed the strings. Glancing up, I saw Dean watching me, with wide eyes and a goofy smile. Trying to ignore him, I switched to an A Major chord, but failed.

"Can you stop looking at me?" I spat, aggravated by my failure to complete a chord progression. "You're distracting me."

"How do you ever expect to perform in front of an audience?"

"I don't expect to, because I'm not going to," I remarked.

"I don't see why not, you're pretty good," Dean replied, trying to flatter me.

"One chord! I played one chord!"

"One chord is enough. I can tell," Dean said. "Go on, continue."

This time, I closed my eyes so I could block Dean out of my mind: D Major, A Major, G Major. I played those three basic chords, again and again, until I was lost in the music and playing away one of my favorite songs. The music consumed me to the point where I had almost forgotten that Dean was watching.

"Crimson and clover, over and over," he lightly sang along near the end of the song. His raspy voice ironically sounded like melted butter. "See, I knew you were good. You're a natural."

Blushing slightly, I said, "Yeah right. But whatever, now you owe me a drum performance."

"Deal," he agreed, while watching me lock the guitar back in its hard case. When I put it back in the cubby, he extended his arm gracefully and said, "After you."

As we walked to the parking lot, I was still experiencing my musical high. My hands tingled from the exhilaration of playing the guitar, my mind felt clear and stress-free, and my lips could only form a smile. My whole body felt weightless as if I was walking on air.

"Hey, happy-go-lucky," Dean called for my attention. "Get over here."

Dean was already straddled onto his navy blue motorcycle. A dark helmet concealed his handsome face, and his leather jacket was now half way zipped.

"You can't be serious," I gapped, mouth wide open. "I can't ride that."

"You can, and you will," Dean insisted, extending a hand that held another helmet.

"If you haven't noticed, I'm wearing a skirt," I replied, pointing to the item of clothing.

"Yeah, I noticed," Dean said, smirking. "Just an excuse. You'll be fine; I promise I won't let anything happen to you."

Nervously, I took the helmet and secured it on my head. With a deep breath, I straddled the back of his bike, feeling awkward and restricted by my skirt.

"Now, hold onto my waist," Dean instructed. I wrapped my arms tightly around his leather clad body. "I'll go nice and easy, okay?"

Pressing the side of my face against his back, I listened as the engine roared as it came to life. The motorcycle accelerated, causing me to hold on tighter and close my eyes in fear. They stayed closed for the first few minutes until I gained enough courage to open them.

Everything looked more realistic; more vivid, and more touchable. It was felt like a scenic journey, enjoying the nature rather than just speeding from Point A to Point B. For once, I was able to see and appreciate the beauty of rural Connecticut; the trees with their withering leaves, the breeze as it whipped through my hair, the sun as it beaded down on my body.

For the first time in a very long time, I felt free.

Unfortunately, we arrived at my house after a short, thirteen-minute ride. Dryly, I got off the bike, pulled off my helmet, and handed it to Dean.

"That wasn't so bad, right?"

"Yeah, thanks for bringing me home in one piece," I said, fluffing my helmet hair.

"Anytime," Dean replied. "Stay golden, Ponyboy."

Dean drove away before I could say anything else. I stood there, in my driveway, wondering if The Outsiders was his favorite book.

CHAPTER 6

"This is bad," Lucy mumbled, after I told her about yesterday's tutoring session before Chemistry started the next day. "This is really, really bad."

"Yeah, yeah, I know," I replied, secretly taking pleasure in her vocal concerns. For once in my life, I was rebelling against something. And boy, did it feel great.

"Why aren't you taking this seriously? If Blake finds out that you're tutoring Dean, he'll freak," she lowered her voice, knowing Blake had a temper. But she had no idea just how bad his temper could get. "You know how he can be."

"Trust me, I know," I replied, rolling my eyes in an attempt to play his jealousy off as typical boyfriend drama.

I was always going to great lengths to keep her safe and blissfully unaware of what was going on. She knew there was trouble in paradise, but I never wanted her to know more than that; it wouldn't be fair to her. I didn't want to put her through knowing that her best friend was being abused and not knowing how to stop it.

Leaving my trail of thoughts and coming back to the conversation, I said: "But I'm willing to take that risk."

"This isn't about tutoring or college credit, this is about Dean," Lucy concluded, raising an eyebrow at me.

"No, it's not," I quickly answered.

Lucy's lips curled into a knowing grin. "It totally is. That's why you're acting so differently. You're totally into him." She gasped. "Don't tell me you want to leave Blake for him!"

"Jesus, Lucy," I snapped. Lucy was always full of wild ideas. She was the type of person that always jumped the gun, skipping out on logic entirely. Her mystified impulsiveness was just another reason why I could never tell her the truth about Blake. "Not even close. I can't believe you'd even suggest something like that."

With a twinkle in her eye, she replied: "Well, can you blame me? I mean, just look at him."

Running a hand over my face, I let out a heavy sigh. I had to shoot this dead, once and for all. Even if she was a little right.

"Lucy, he's just a guy, who I happen to be friendly with. What, are girls not allowed to have guys as friends anymore?"

"Not when the guy could pass as a model."

"You know, when he's actually not that good looking if you look at his face closely," I lied, trying to get her off my case.

Admittedly, it was really hard to force myself to not feel a little something towards him. Good looks aside; he had a certain appeal that drew me in. Dean represented what I wanted, but didn't have: confidence, spontaneity, freedom.

Dean was his own person. He didn't care what people thought, or how people wanted him to act — he only cared about he wanted, and how he wanted to be. That attitude attracted me more than anything else.

But reality kept me in check. True life constantly reminded me that due to the circumstances, I should resist any sort of temptation I had towards him.

Besides, the tutoring sessions meant more to me than just spending an hour or two with Dean.

"Just promise me you won't bite off more than you can chew?" Lucy asked. "I get the sense that trouble follows him."

"Promise," I swore, just as the bell rang.

Everybody took their seats, as Mr. Richards started writing on the whiteboard. Every seat was occupied, except for Dean's. I couldn't help but wonder if he was skipping, but then directed my attention towards my teacher's lecture.

Twenty minutes into class, Dean walked in, sporting a black eye.

"Nice of you to join us," my teacher said, his eyes focused on the obvious bruise. But he didn't dare ask about it, nobody did.

It bugged me, it really did. Having my fair share of black eyes, I was desperate to find out the cause of his. But I knew I shouldn't pry into his private life, just like he didn't pry into mine when he found me bleeding in the parking lot.

The bell rang, signally all of us to flock out of the room at once. Lucy and I started walking down the science wing, when someone called out my name.

"Riley! Wait up," Dean yelled, racing down the hall. Suddenly, I felt uncomfortable, knowing dozens of girls were glaring at me.

"I'll see you later," Lucy said, glancing at Dean and then back at me.

"Hey Teach," Dean said, slightly out of breath. "How about another study session today afterschool?"

"If you want, sure," I replied in a pleasantly surprised tone before starting to walk again.

Dean kept pace with me. "I do. Where are you headed? I'll walk you to class."

"I have a free period," I muttered, biting down on my lip.

"Right, right, junior parking lot," Dean recalled. "Let me walk you there."

Imagining Blake's reaction to seeing me with Dean brought me to say, "That's okay. I don't want to make you late to class."

"I've already been late to one class. Might as well keep my track record," Dean replied. His persistence was puzzling to me. But I had a feeling that I would never fully understand Dean Marks.

"Really, you don't have to."

"I don't have to, but I want to," Dean insisted, stopping to turn and look directly at me. My heart jumped a little at the fact that he wanted to do all of these things with me. But I told myself over and over again to not read too much into it.

I looked away and started walking again. "It's fine, I'll see you after school." My voice sounded a little harsher than I wanted, but it did the trick.

Thankfully, I got the parking lot before Blake did. Standing in the cold for a few minutes was much better than having Blake lash out at me for making him wait.

Blake came just as my legs were starting to get numb. I quickly panicked, remembering yesterday's threat.

"Hi."

"Hey," I replied, crossing my arms around my chest.

"Let's just forget about yesterday, and move on, okay?" Blake extended his arms out, waiting for me to embrace him. That was the complete opposite of his "I never forget" rant, but I had no complaints. I forced myself to wrap my arms around him, knowing it was best please him and avoid any confrontations.

It was days like where I felt bi-polar. In just one hour, I had gone from taking a ride on the wild side to playing on the safe side. I had taken one step forward, and one step back.

Blake and I spent our free period at the local diner. We ate some brunch and order malt milkshakes. Blake spent most of the time talking about the football team's new strategies, while I pretended to listen. After we paid the bill, Blake drove us back to the school.

Everything seemed to be going okay. For once, we were able to survive 45 minutes together without fighting. Unfortunately, we couldn't survive another 15.

"So, how did that thing go yesterday?" Blake asked, after he was parked in front of the school.

"Fine." I wasn't in the mood for this. My hand reached for the door handle, but Blake quickly hit the lock button and grabbed my arm.

"Are you still not going to tell me what it was?"

"Look it's nothing okay? I thought we agreed to forget about it," I stated.

"Well, I changed my mind," Blake said, his grip around my arm growing tighter.

"Well, you can't do that," I replied. "Please, Blake, let me go."

Blake whipped his arm around, striking his fist against my cheek. "You know, you do this to yourself. If you didn't disobey and lie to me, I wouldn't have to teach you a lesson. When will you ever learn?"

Instead of letting the pain bring me to tears, I channeled it into anger. With all of my physical and emotional strength, I used my free arm to sock Blake square in the face. He instantly released his grip, covering his bloody nose with his hands.

"I'll learn as soon as you learn that I'm not your personal punching bag," I snapped, unlocking the car door and slamming it shut for emphasis. The power felt great . . . I had finally done it.

But I hadn't won yet.

Just as I was storming away, Blake got out of his car and stalked after me. He was decreasing the distance between us, so I tried to pick up my speed by running. However, my ballet flats caused me to trip and fall, hitting the cold pavement, scraping at face.

"Not so powerful now, are we?" Blake sneered, peering down at me as I laid helplessly on the ground. "Get up."

My arms shook as I pushed myself up. When I was on my feet again, I took sly steps backwards.

"Don't you dare come near me," I threatened. But the fear and weakness in my voice caused Blake to not take me seriously. "I mean it, don't you ever touch me again."

Blake took a slow step forward, while I took a slow step back. His eyes filled with bestial fire, ready to attack. This was it, I was dead meat. Just as I closed my eyes in fear, the bell rang.

My eyes shot open as his eyes simmered down. We watched as students with free periods burst out the front doors and into the parking lot, ready to leave campus for an hour.

"We're not finished," he growled, before storming towards the school.

I sighed with relief, knowing I was safe for now. The cheek had struck was sticky and stinging from the cold, nippy air. I rushed past the crowd of people, hiding the side of my face, trying to navigate my way to the nurse's office.

Just as I was about to enter, somebody coming out of her office slammed right into me, causing me to keel over.

Dean, who had been holding an ice bag to his black eye, helped me back up.

He held my chin, turning my face to the side so he could get a better look at my scratch. "What the hell did you do this time?"

"What do you think?"

"I want to think that you fell again, but . . ."

"Well, I did," I said, before he could make up his own conclusion.

"Why is it that you always fall during your free period? As I see it, you don't fall any other time of the day," Dean replied, skeptically.

"Just an unlucky hour I guess," I lied, covering up the truth. But I could tell Dean didn't buy it, which was my cue to leave. "Now if you don't mind, I'd like to get this taken care of."

Dean shrugged, and opened the door for me. Instead of closing the door behind me, he followed me into the nurse's office.

"What are you still doing here?"

"Hey, I just want to make sure you're alright," Dean replied. I rolled my eyes, knowing that wasn't the real reason.

I greeted the nurse, while Dean plopped down onto one of the plastic chairs in the sitting room. He slouched back, putting the ice back on his eye.

"Oh my," Nurse Zeda exclaimed, horrified.

"How bad does it look?" I asked, thrown off at her large reaction.

"On a scale from 1 to 10, it looks like some zombie just clawed off your skin," Dean called from the waiting room.

"Gross," I muttered to the nurse. I called back to him playfully, "And just for the record, that wasn't as witty as you think it was."

"It sounded better in my head," Dean called back.

The gash didn't look that bad once Nurse Zeda scrubbed the dried blood away.

"I don't know what you want to do, Honey," Nurse Zeda started. "I could either put a bandage on and send you black to class, or you could just wait here until the bleeding stops."

"She'll wait here," Dean said, coming up to us.

Nurse Zeda exchanged glances with both of us, shook her head, and walked back to her desk.

"Dean, I can't afford to miss class," I urged.

"And you can't afford to explain the reason why you have a huge band-aid on the side of your face to everyone," Dean replied.

"I told you . . . I fell."

"We both know that's not the real reason," Dean dropped his voice. He pulled me into the sitting room, and we both sat down. "If you tell me how you really got your cut, I'll tell you how I really got my black eye."

I took a deep breath. He trusted me enough to let me into his private life, but did I trust him enough to let him into mine? After all, I had only known him for a few days.

I found my answer, deep inside his dark, caring, sincere eyes.

CHAPTER 7

I opened my mouth to speak, but swallowed back my words.

"I'm sorry, Dean," I whispered, in fear. "I don't think I can say . . ."

Avoiding his eyes, I left, slamming the door behind me, and racing to the closest bathroom. Hanging over the sink, I splashed my face with cold water, and took deep breaths.

Why did I always do this to myself? Why did I let my fear get the best of me? Why couldn't I just trust him?

Believe me, I wanted to tell him. Something about him made me feel secure. But, as usual, I was afraid . . . I was afraid of being let down, hurt, and betrayed.

After the cut on my face stopped bleeding and my breathing patterns went back to normal, I left the bathroom, and headed back to class.

My classes dragged on, the minutes slowly passing by as the words of the teachers blended into an inarticulate mush. This time, I didn't even bother trying to focus. I just sat there, staring at the blank page of notebook paper on my desk, scorning myself for always acting like a fool.

When the last bell rang, I was not among the students who were relieved to finally leave school. A crucial decision was to be made.

I couldn't face Dean . . . not after how I behaved. And unless I wanted to receive a full-blown beating, going home with Blake was out of the question.

For the first time in months, I took the bus home. The chaos of the bus in the afternoon was much worse than in the morning. But considering the consequences of the other options, I couldn't complain too much.

When I finally got home, I headed directly for my bedroom. Slipping my hand under my mattress, I pulled out my red leather journal. After opening up to a fresh page, I tapped my pen against my teeth, and tried to brain storm what to write about.

The doorbell rang just as an idea popped into my head. The digital clock on my desk told me it was far too early for Charlie to be home. Plodding down the stairs to the front door, I pondered at who it could be.

"Where were you?" Blake sneered the minute I opened the door.

I tried slamming the door closed, but Blake pressed against it, forcing it back open. Enough was enough.

"Go away, Blake," I spat, trying to push the door. "You're trespassing private property."

"Yeah, what are you going to do about it? Call the cops? Call my father?" Laughing, Blake pressed his back against the door.

He gave the door an extra shove, causing me to stagger backwards and fall onto the carpet. Blake circled around me, his eyes gleaming with victory, and his lips curled in mockery.

"Why do you keep trying? Why do you feel the need to keep fighting against me? You're not going to win," Blake said, with self-righteousness. "You know, this is only to benefit you. I'm trying to teach you how to become a loyal, respectable girlfriend. I do this only out of love."

"If you loved me like you say you do," I croaked through the tears. "You wouldn't hurt me."

"I only hurt you because you force me too. You bring it upon yourself. Now, if you were the good little girl that you were supposed to be, then I wouldn't have to result to such actions," Blake replied waltzing around the living room, oblivious to his vicious, inhumane words.

"You are a sick bastard," I growled, filled with rage. "I hope you burn in hell."

"What did you say to me?" Blake said, snapping around to face me with beady eyes. "Get up, now."

I glared up with him, pouting my lip, and shaking my head. Blake, with speedy, carnal movement, lurched down and pulled me up by my hair. He punched, he slapped, he beat, he kicked, he pummeled, he destroyed until he was fully satisfied.

My body ached with unspeakable pain. Every inch of my skin felt on fire, every internal organ throbbed, every limb shook with feebleness.

"Get in the car," Blake ordered, pushing my limp body forward. "I don't want your brother to come home and see this."

My legs weakly carried my frail body down the driveway. Blake gave me another shove, trying to get me to move faster.

Blake pushed me against the side of the truck, the metal pressing into my back. He opened the passenger door, and tried shoving me in. But I fought with every last bit of strength I had left. Getting in that car meant giving up any last bit of hope and freedom. If I got in that car, he could take me anywhere and do anything.

"Get in," Blake roared, grabbing onto my waist and dragging my body. I gripped onto the side of the door, my arms resisting. I screamed, in pain, in fear, and in need of any help. All I needed was for one neighbor to hear, come outside, and put an end to this.

Blake grabbed onto my neck, chocking me so I couldn't produce any sound. But not even Blake could muffle out the noise that was quickly approaching. As I lost more oxygen, the loud, mechanic rumble grew louder. My head grew dizzy as the noise came closer and closer, until it was next to me . . . and then it stopped.

Before I knew it, somebody was shouting. Blake let go, causing me to keel over as I inhaled fresh oxygen. As my vision recovered, I saw somebody pummel Blake into the cold, black pavement. Blake put up a fight, throwing punches back, but he was causing little damage.

My eyes were glued to them, as they fought until Blake could no longer go on. He laid limp on the ground, panting as the blood gushed from his skin.

Dean got up, wiped his bloody hands on his jeans, and came over to me.

"Riley? Are you okay?" Dean asked, kneeling down at my side. I raised my hand to my feverish forehead, doubting reality.

"Who the hell do you think you are, talking to my girlfriend? You don't even know her," Blake roared, rising to his feet.

"I'm not your girlfriend anymore," I muttered, breathing heavily, as I stood up. "And he does know me. I'm his tutor."

Despite his limp, Blake stormed towards me, filled with hatred. Dean quickly stepped in front of me, blocking Blake's path.

Blake clenched his jaw. "Get out of my way."

"You've got to get through me first."

"Fine," Blake said, balling his fists together.

Just as Blake swung his arm around, gaining momentum, Dean swiftly delivered a sharp, powerful punch to Blake's face, knocking him down with one shot.

"How did you do that?" I whispered in awe. Blake, a man who could not be defeated, just got his ass kicked . . . twice. Dean simply shrugged.

For the last time, Blake pushed himself up. "You'll regret this Riley, I swear you will. As for you, new kid, you better watch your back. My father will be hearing about this, so choose your actions very carefully."

"Oh, I'm so scared," Dean said, sarcastically. "Fuck off."

Wiping his bloody chin, Blake hopped into his pick up truck, and sped off.

After Blake's car was out of sight, Dean whispered, "Come on, let's get you inside and cleaned up."

Dean linked his arm around mine, helping me inside. He sat me down on the kitchen counter, and dabbed away at my cuts with a warm wash cloth. I let my eyes close, feeling his warm breath as he gently scrubbed my sensitive skin.

"Why did you come?"

"Well, you didn't show up for our tutoring session, so I wanted to make sure you were okay," Dean said, ringing out the wash cloth.

"Thank you, I don't know what would have happened if you didn't," I murmured, shivering at the thought.

Dean came back over and began to wash the cuts on my arms and legs, giving me a closer look at his face. His black eye looked much better, but a few minor scratches had been added to his chiseled face.

"Why didn't you tell me?" Dean asked, his dark eyes filled with hurt.

I had anticipated this conversation, but now I couldn't think of anything to say.

"I don't know . . . I haven't even told my best friend of 5 years. Can you blame me? I barely know you."

"So then get to know me," he replied. "I want to get to know you too, but I can't do that if you won't let me in."

"I'm sorry, Dean," I mumbled, biting down on my lip. But it wasn't enough. After all he did for me, I owed him much more than one lousy apology. "I put up these barriers to protect myself."

"It's not a matter of becoming vulnerable," Dean said, wiping the blood between my fingers. "It's a matter of who you become vulnerable too."

Just then, we heard the front door open. Charlie waltzed into the kitchen with his earphones in, humming to himself as he grabbed a snack from the pantry, completely oblivious to our presence. When he turned around, he jumped at the sight of us.

"Who's this?" Charlie first asked, ripping out his earphones.

"Charlie, this is my friend, Dean." Dean helped me down from the kitchen counter, then went over to shake my little brother's hand.

"Nice to meet you," Dean said, charismatically.

Charlie gave him an awkward smile, then peered over to look at me. "Is Blake coming over too?"

Dean and I exchanged glances. "No, probably not. Charlie, Blake won't be around much anymore."

"Why not?" Charlie asked, ruffling his chocolate brown hair.

"We broke up. It just wasn't working out," I muttered, softening the truth. Deep down, I knew Charlie deserved to know. But I just couldn't bring myself to tell him.

Charlie said, taking a bit into his cookie. "Riley, why are you all bloody? Mom's going to flip."

"She tripped over one of the hurdles on the track during gym class," Dean lied, covering for me. "That's why I took her home to get her cleaned up."

"Classic Riley," my brother muttered before heading up the stairs.

"Thank you," I said, once I heard my brother's bedroom door shut.

"It's the least I could do, considering how bad of a liar you are," Dean lightly teased. "I'm assuming he doesn't know the truth about Blake?"

I shook my head, filled with everlasting guilt. "No, he doesn't. Neither does my mother. My dad is the only one in my family that knows."

Dean headed over to the sink, and started rinsing the wash cloth. "And what does he think?"

"Well, he's a criminal lawyer, so he's seen similar situations that have ended badly . . . but he's working to find a solution. Its pretty tough on him though," I replied.

That was the understatement of the century. Everyday, my father feared for my life. He carried that burden to work, to home, to bed, constantly worrying about what would happen if one mistake was made.

Hopefully now, it would become easier -- for all of us.

CHAPTER 8

"Working hard or hardly working?" My father asked, dropping his coat and briefcase onto an empty chair.

My father's eyes glazed over the leather-cladded, tattooed boy sitting across from me. But my father was not one to judge a person by their cover . . . that was my mother.

"Hey Dad," I started, glancing at Dean, then back to my father. "This is my friend, Dean."

Dean immediately shot up, approached my father, and shook his hand eagerly.

"It's great to meet you, sir," Dean said, eager to make a good impression on my father.

"You too, Dean," my father warmly replied. "How was your day?"

Dean and I glanced at each other, silently debating who should drop the bomb.

"Dad?" The shrill of his name echoed through the dining room. I stood up, pushed the hair that covered my face away, rolled up my sleeves, and walked towards them. The fluorescent ceiling lights illuminated every cut, bruise, and scab. "Blake and I broke up."

My dad scanned my body with his eyes, horrified by the damage done. He looked back at Dean, his concerned eyes fixed on the black eye and minor scratches. Dad's eyebrows rose, as if he had a realization, connecting all of the pieces together.

"This is a good thing, right?" I asked. "We won't have to worry about him anymore."

But my father didn't seem to think that at all. In fact, he looked more troubled than ever before, as if he was holding something inside. My heart dropped into my stomach, afraid to know what was running through my father's mind.

"Come with me," Dad ordered, his voice low and cold. "I want to show you guys something."

Dean and I followed him up the stairs, into his office. We stood in the corner, as my father pulled out law book after law book, and piled files and documents into a mountain on his desk. We watched silently as my father furiously flipped through the pages, sometimes ripping the pages by accident.

"The day I found out about this . . ." My father started, vigorously shuffling through loose papers. He picked up a book, tore through the pages, and then threw it over his shoulder. "I started searching for a way out of this mess. I couldn't just call the cops, considering his father's position. Not to mention, you never know how someone in his sort of mindset will react. We certainly couldn't sue him and file for a restraining order . . . seeing how Darcy Buhmann, Michelle Castillo, Laura Aceves and many more women of abuse all did that and ended up dead because of it." My father ran his hand through his slick hair, causing it to stick up in different directions.

I wiped away the tear that ran down my face as I watch my father rip apart his office and mutter to himself as he searched endlessly for an answer to all of our problems. I had caused my father to crack and crumble to pieces. This great lawyer I call my father was trained to be reasonable, calm, and level-headed under pressure.

But my problem, my stress, my burden had broken him, filling me with unbearable guilt.

"What did Blake say when you broke up with him?" My father now rested on the floor, surrounded by his mess. My father was never this unkept; his blazer was off, his tie was loose, his hair was messy, and his face was flushed with anxiety.

Because the sight of my father paralyzed my mouth, Dean answered for me. "He said Riley would live to regret this, and that I had to watch my back."

"Oh great . . ." My father muttered as he crawled to his bottom bookshelf. Dean crossed over to me, and placed his hand on the small of my back.

"I can't do this to him . . . I can't stand to see him like this," I whispered, tripping over my words.

"Riley, it's going to be okay. I'll take care of this," he whispered back, reassuring me. I bit down on my bottom lip, nodded, and trusted his words.

"Mr. Jennings?" Dean slowly walked towards my father, crouched down, and looked him straight in the eye. He spoke in a clear yet soft tone. "What you're doing is great . . . but I don't think we need to solve everything today."

My father stopped his search, and looked up at Dean. "You don't?"

At that very moment, my father seemed so young, so naïve, so incredibly helpless. The two of them had switched roles; where Dean was the wise, older man and Dad was the impulsive, fearful teenager.

"I don't. I think if we can just handle things day by day, we can gradually figure everything out." Dean took the book out of my father's hand, and gave him a modest smile. It was suddenly clear to me that Dean had a natural talent for comforting people.

Something about him made people feel safe, like no matter how bad things might be, everything would work out in the end.

The crimson color escaped my father's face, as he took deep breaths, slowly recovering from his panic attack.

"What exactly do you suggest?" My father asked.

"That every day before, during, and after school, I watch out for Riley and protect her if Blake tries anything," Dean said, glancing back for my approval.

I was caught off guard, dumbfounded by the thought of being with him every day. Was I ready for this? It was one thing to tutor him once or twice a week, and another to spend every waking day with him.

But what was Dean thinking? That perplexed me the most.

I mean, I just couldn't figure out why he felt so prompted to help me. He could have just turned a blind eye like the rest of the world. I mean, he hardly knew me for Christ Sake, and yet here he was, consoling my father and offering his protection. The better I got to know Dean Marks, the more he turned into an enigma.

There must have been something deeper inside of him that was compelling him, something from his past. I thought about his mother and wondered if he had sisters. Still, it didn't quite add up.

My eyes drifted to my shambolic father, who was gradually returning back to his normal state of mind. Nevertheless, it was undeniable that we needed Dean's help. Reluctantly, I nodded back at Dean, giving him my sign of acceptance. He smiled with his eyes, thanking me for trusting him.

Dean continued. "Riley and I will dig up some dirt on Blake overtime, and together we can all figure out a way to take him down."

My father looked deep in thought, as he tried to tame his unruly hair. "And you think this will work?"

Dean looked at me, then back at my father. "I do, Mr. Jennings. I really do." He bent down, and offered his hand, helping my father up.

My father brushed himself off, and whispered, "Thank you for taking care of my daughter."

"No problem," Dean said, beaming brightly.

"Look at the mess I made," my father said, scanning the clutter in his office. "Your mother is not going to be happy when she sees this."

"We can help you clean," Dean offered.

"No, no, you've already helped enough today," my father replied. He sounded exhausted, as if all his energy had escaped from his body. "I need a shower. I'll take care of this later." My father maneuvered his way out of his office and said, "Thank you again, Dean. You don't know how much this means."

My father left, leaving the two of us stranded in his chaotic office. Moments passed by, as we soaked in everything that had just happened.

"You've been awfully quiet this whole time," Dean said, finally breaking the silence.

"It's been a long day," I shrugged, "Thank you so much, for everything. You don't have to do this."

"Well, I'm just glad I can help," Dean modestly said. "I don't have to, but I want to."

"No, really. We couldn't do any of this without you," I replied. My words lingered in the air, as Dean just stared at me with his deep, brown eyes. "Please, at least stay for dinner. It's the least we can do."

"No, I should probably get home," Dean said, walking towards the door. "My mom probably needs my help making her famous lasagna."

My stomach growled, desperate for food. "That sounds delicious."

"Oh, it is. My mom's a great cook," Dean boasted, as we walked down the stairs. Once we were downstairs, Dean gathered his belongings and headed for the front door. "Thanks for being such a trooper, Riley. I know this must be really tough for you. Just promise me, you'll stay strong throughout this - no matter what happens, no matter what it takes."

Strong? Of course, he was asking for the one thing I've always struggled with. The inconsistency of my strength was evident - with random, short bursts of courage.

But for the sake of Dean, Dad, and me, I would try to be the toughest, strongest girl I could be.

"I promise," I whispered, secretly hoping that I wouldn't let him down.

Chapter 9

I wasn't able to sleep that night. My mind kept wandering about how everything was going to change. Tomorrow marked a new chapter in my life, and that intimidated me.

Because sleep was out of the question, I searched for something to occupy my time. None of my books seemed appealing, nothing good was on television, and my mind was too overly exhausted to write in my journal. So I decided to do some laundry and organize my closet.

Filling the washing machine with a load of whites, I suddenly remembered Dean's blood stained, white linen handkerchief. I ran back into my room, removed the cloth from the front pocket of my backpack, and headed back into the laundry room. Even with crimson stains, the handkerchief was still beautiful and delicate. My fingers traced along the mysterious BK, still mesmerized by the soft, surreptitious lettering.

At this point, Dean knew all of my secrets, but I was still in the dark about his. Let alone, it was not my place to pry. Dean didn't pry; he just happened to be in the wrong place at the right time.

I scrubbed the handkerchief with some bleach stain remover, threw it into the washing machine, and turned it on. Afterward,

I went back into my room and started rummaging through my wardrobe.

Productively, I worked my through the closet, organizing it by garment, color, and season. I was almost done when I came across a pair of jeans I had never seen before.

Holding up the dark denim material, I tried to remember the last time I had bought jeans. It had been months, years, since I had last considered wearing something other than a skirt. Examining them, I assumed that Lucy must have left them at my house, and they somehow got mixed into my laundry.

Curiously, I stood up and tried the jeans on. They were too long, so I casually cuffed them at my ankles. Other than that, they fitted like a gem, hugging and accentuating my curves.

And that's when I decided that I would wear them to school. If everything was else was changing in my life, why couldn't my clothes change? Sure, it was just a small attire adjustment, but it was symbolic. For once, Blake couldn't stop me from wearing what I wanted; nobody could.

The blare of my alarm clock woke me up the next morning, but it sounded more distant than usual. As my eyes fluttered open, I realized I had slept on the floor, using my cashmere sweater as a pillow and my pea coat as a blanket. Most of my clothes were still scattered in piles around my room, so I must have fallen asleep before finishing.

After my shower, I got dressed, sliding on my newly discovered jeans and my black blazer. Before heading downstairs, I headed into the laundry room and pulled out Dean's freshly cleaned handkerchief.

As I ate my morning bagel, I started tugging at my jeans, feeling out of my comfort zone. I was about to go upstairs and change when Dean arrived. Disappointed, I slugged my backpack over my shoulder and headed out to my driveway.

"Good morning," Dean greeted, embracing the morning sunshine. "It's a brand new day."

"A new day, a new beginning," I muttered nervously, as I approached him.

Dean peered over his aviators and said, "Are you wearing jeans?"

My cheeks reddened with embarrassment, and I felt even more awkward than ever before.

"Uh ..." I looked down at my cuffed ankles, knowing how stupid I looked. "Yeah, I should probably go change, if you don't mind waiting."

"No, don't," Dean insisted, smiling brightly as he examined me from head to toe. "I think it looks great."

"Yeah?"

"Yeah, totally," Dean said, straddling his bike. Holding out the extra helmet, he said, "Hop on."

Riding on his bike was just as great as I remembered. Only this time, when I separated my legs, the world couldn't see up my underwear. We arrived at school just minutes before the bell.

"Here," I pulled the handkerchief out of my bag, "this is yours. I cleaned it and everything."

Dean looked down at the cloth in my hand, then back up at me. He almost looked . . . hurt.

"I told you to keep it," he whispered, as we walked up the front steps of the school. "I want you to have it."

"Please, just take it," I begged.

Dean silently walked for a few minutes. Then, he stopped in his path and took the handkerchief out of my hand. His fingers lightly grazed my skin, sending electric shocks through my body.

"So I hope you do know that I'll be walking to you every class," Dean said, holding the door open for me.

"I'm aware of that," I replied, stepping into our chemistry class.

"Try not to get too sick of me, okay?" Dean gave me a crooked smile before taking his seat.

Lucy approached me as fast as she could, following me as I sat down.

"What's going on? Everyone in school is talking about the breakup. What happened? And why did you walk in with the new kid?" As she took a moment to catch her breath, she looked down at my pants. "And why are you wearing my jeans?"

"Lucy," I murmured, rubbing my throbbing temple. Lucy could go on spinning tangents if nobody ever stopped it. "Please, slow down. It is way to early in the morning."

"Sorry but you're not telling me anything," she said, crossing her arms in protest. "Do you know how awkward it was to be the last to find out that my best friend is single now?"

"I'm sorry," I muttered, sighing. "I've got a lot on my mind."

"And the best way to deal with that is to tell your best friend what's bothering you."

"Miss Wilde," my teacher called, "take your seat."

I moaned, "I'll tell you later."

"You better," she demanded, walking to her desk.

The lesson felt like it would never end; every minute that passed was another minute that Lucy spent in the dark. But I had gone this far without her knowing the truth. Over the past year, I experienced waves of guilt when I thought about how I was hiding such a big secret from my best friend. I constantly had to remind myself that keeping her out of it was the right thing to do, even though she probably would have insisted otherwise.

The remorse was even stronger today, knowing I had told a near-stranger about it before telling her.

"So that's it? It's over," Lucy said after I gave her a recap full of lies once chemistry class was over. "Just like that?"

"Well, yeah I guess so. . ." I grumbled.

Lucy looked across the room, where Dean was sitting, patiently waiting for the bell to ring. "And, what's happening with Dean?"

"Nothing . . . he just has offered to give me rides to and from school since Blake won't be anymore, in exchange for my tutoring services."

"I knew it!" Lucy exclaimed. "This was about Dean the whole time, I totally called it! I knew you were starting to like him. You ended things with Blake because of Dean."

"Lucy, stop it," I demanded, starting to feel sick to my stomach. Lucy, with her dashing thought pattern and wild imagination, could make my head spin. "Do you seriously think I would do something like that? I wasn't happy with Blake -- end of story. And do you really think I'm ready to jump into another relationship?"

"Whatever you say . . . regardless, just be careful around him, okay? He may seem pretty nice but I get the feeling that trouble follows him."

The bell rang, causing everyone to stampede out of the classroom. Dean joined us, lingering by my side as we walked down the crowded hallway.

"I guess I'll see you guys at lunch," Lucy said, nodding to Dean before she headed in a different direction.

"Everything alright?" He asked

"Yeah . . . of course, why do you ask?"

"Just checking. You looked a little uneasy," Dean concluded, as he took the books out of my hands and carried them.

"Yeah, I'm fine, just stressed," I replied, waving my hand in the air.

"Don't be, everything's going to be okay," Dean said, in a soft, raspy voice. "The worst is over."

Except it wasn't, it was just beginning. Neither of us knew what to expect from Blake. He was a wild card, as many psychopaths tend to be. For all we knew, he could have some mischievous, brilliant plan brewing that could ruin us both.

"Yeah, I hope so," I muttered, doubtfully.

"You have a free period now, right? Do you want me to skip class and stay with you?"

"What kind of tutor would I be if I made you miss class? No, I'll be okay. I think I'll just go to the library and study."

"You sure?"

"Yeah, I'm positive," I said, taking back my books. "I'll see you next period, okay?"

"Okay," Dean said, facing me. "Stay out of trouble."

When I got to the library, I sat at an empty wooden desk and cracked open my AP U.S. History textbook. As I read, the corner of my eye caught a glimpse of blond hair. Through my peripheral vision, I watched as the blond hair moved from the bookshelves to my table.

"Where's your big, strong protector?"

"Go away, Blake," I hissed, refusing to look up at him. "Just leave me alone."

"If you think I'm going to ... if you think I ever will, you're wrong. Don't think you can get rid of me so easily," he spat. "I'm not giving up."

"Well, I'm not giving in," I replied firmly, staring at him with firm, fierce eyes.

"Oh, so now that you've got yourself a little bodyguard, and put on a pair of jeans, you think you're some kind of tough girl," Blake said, mockery in his voice. "No matter how hard you try, no matter how much you pretend, you will always be the same weak, pathetic individual that you've always been."

Even when he wasn't my boyfriend, he still treated me like I was worthless. He had no right, no control, and no ownership over me. He meant absolutely nothing to me.

"Don't sit there and act like you know me . . . you don't know who I am, you know the girl who you forced me to be."

"You are nothing, nobody without me, so don't try to fool yourself," he spat, clenching his teeth. "You better watch out, and so should your little boy toy, because you don't know who you're messing with."

"It's funny how you act all high and mighty when Dean is ten times the man you'll ever be. I thought he proved that yesterday when he beat the shit out of you."

Blake laughed devilishly. "You really don't know anything, do you? Maybe you're not as smart as I thought you were . . . I'm not the bad guy, he is. Maybe if you did your research, like an intelligent human being would, you wouldn't be so lost right now."

My heart pounded loudly, thumping in my ears. "What . . . what are you talking about?"

Blake shrugged, satisfied with the mayhem he had created. I watched him as he stormed out of the library, stunned by his brutal, shocking words.

CHAPTER 10

"Dean, please, it's okay."

After school, I told Dean about the intervention I had with Blake in the library. However, I made the crucial decision to leave out what Blake had said about Dean; just in case it was a false accusation that would only create more, unnecessary drama. Besides, how was I supposed to know if Blake was telling the truth or trying to mess with me?

"No, Riley, it's not. He can't do that to you," Dean said. "I knew it was a bad idea to leave you."

"Dean, you can't always watch and protect me . . . I'm going to have to do some things on my own," I said, asserting my independence.

Yes, I couldn't deny that I needed Dean's help. But I was trying to change, trying to be strong - fully depending on somebody else was the opposite of what I was aiming for.

"I know, I just worry."

We were walking to the junior parking lot, when an army of strongly built men blocked our path. The football jocks circled around us, as Blake stepped forward from the pack.

Dean grabbed my waist, and pulled himself in front of me, blocking me off from Blake.

"Isn't this cute? The rebellious, dimwitted delinquent protecting the modest, insecure brainiac." Blake clapped his hands together in a slow rhythm, while the jocks laughed in unison. "What an unconventional pair."

"Get out of our way," Dean growled.

"Tempting offer . . ." Blake rubbed his chin. "But I think I'm going to take a pass."

Anger and hatred pulsed through my veins. The pain he had caused me started to rebuild inside of me, growing stronger as the memories fled back.

"You're an asshole! What you did to me makes you a sick, worthless, ignorant pig! I hate you, do you hear me, I hate you!"

Sobbing, I lunged forward, trying to claw at his face and give him a taste of his own medicine. But Dean wrapped his arms around my waist, and held me back.

"It's not worth it, don't sink to his level," Dean cooed in my ear. "Let's just go."

"Not so fast," Blake ordered, snapping his fingers at the jocks, causing them close off the gaps. "It appears the tough guy doesn't want to fight us. Do I sense fear?"

"No, it's just not a fair fight," Dean said, scanning the six football players that faced us.

"And what will your excuse be when your Black Knights are standing beside you?"

Dean quickly looked at me, his eyes filled with panic.

"There won't be one," he murmured to Blake. Dean lightly tugged on my arm, and pushed through the blockade. "Let's go, Riley."

Dean stormed forward, desperate to get farther and farther away. I lingered a few steps behind him, slowly processing everything that had happened. But as much as I thought about it, I couldn't seem to understand it at all. I was lost, confused, dumbfounded, just like Blake had said.

"Dean," I called to him, stopped in my tracks. "What's going on? What was Blake talking about? What was all of that Black Knight stuff?"

Dean slowly turned around, and hung his head down. He walked towards me, his combat boots crunching in the gravel.

"It's nothing . . . just forget about it," Dean murmured.

"Dean, please, whatever it is, you can tell me," I assured, the desire to know filling me up.

"You wouldn't understand . . ." Dean shook his head and turned on his heel. I could feel he was pulling away from me as he continued walking steps ahead of me.

"Try me," I whispered. "I opened up to you. I can't imagine it's any worse than what you know about me."

Dean whipped his head around and looked at me with exasperated eyes. "Riley, I said forget about it," he snapped, with fiery frustration in his voice.

Fear silenced me. I had never seen Dean get so . . . angry.

Dumbfounded for words, I followed him to the bike without commenting.

The ride home felt longer than usual. I did my best to do as he asked and forget about it. But the thought lingered in my head, no matter how hard I tried to push it out. I was not only completely baffled and lost in confusion, but I was slightly hurt. In a way, I felt foolish for opening up to him thinking that he could do the same. I felt naked and vulnerable, while Dean was protected by the clothing of his secrets.

For being the smartest girl in school, I felt like the biggest idiot in the world.

"Are we okay?" Dean asked, opening the front door for me.

I nodded, uneasily. "I mean . . . I suppose."

Dean lowered his eyes at me in disbelief. "You know, you're a terrible liar."

I took a deep breath. "Well to be honest, I think it's pretty unfair that you know everything about me," I admitted before lowering my voice. "And I know nothing about you."

Dean reached out, put his hands on arms and leaned in a bit closer. "You know everything you need to know about me, Riley. Everything else is unimportant."

Keeping my gaze steady, I replied: "This whole Black Knight thing seems pretty important."

Dean let go, and took a step back while letting out a heavy sigh. "It is and it isn't. But I promise, you'll know soon, when the time is right. I won't leave you in the dark."

"Why is now not the right time?" I asked, with an impatient tone.

One of my biggest pet peeves was not knowing all of the answers. I guess that's why I always pushed myself in school to study for exams until I knew the material like the back of my hand.

"Because it's been a long day for both of us," he murmured. "And right now, the last thing you need is one more thing to worry about."

I looked up at him with puzzled eyes. "Is this something I should be worried about?"

He gave me a sweet, half smile. "No, never. And you will know. Soon. I promise," Dean murmured.

I let out a sigh, taking a minute to process this. There was nothing more to be said about this; it was what it was and I just had to accept that. All I could do was wait for him to be ready.

"Okay," I eventually whispered.

His half smile turned into a toothy grin. "Hey, if you agree to go out with me on Saturday night, I'll tell you then."

Baffled that the conversation had taken a complete 180 degree turn, I cocked my head to the side. "What?"

Dean ran a nervous hand through his dark hair, and began to stammer a bit. "I've got tickets to see The Shins . . . I don't know if you like them, but I think it would be fun to do something different for once. Plus, we both could use the distraction. And hey, you like music and stuff so maybe you'd like to go with me . . ."

"As friends?" I blurted out, immediately regretting the question.

Dean's voice dropped slightly as his smile faded. "Yeah sure . . . if you want."

"Okay," I said, taking awkward pauses. Not trying to read too much into it, I simply said: "Sounds fun."

"Yeah?" He asked, slightly doubting himself.

"Yeah."

"Okay, cool," Dean replied, scratching the back of his neck.

We exchanged awkward glances, both of us still a bit uneasy from the previous conversation. I don't think either of us knew what the hell we were doing. But maybe it was better to not give it a second thought, just move on and say fuck it all.

"Well, I should probably get home. I'll see you tomorrow," Dean murmured, before walking down my driveway.

I watched him for a few moments, then proceeded to find my house keys. I closed the front door after opening it, then slowly slid down to floor, trying to process everything.

Why couldn't life just be easy?

CHAPTER 11

"I knew it! I told you so!" Lucy's exclamation was muffled out by the clamor in the cafeteria. "He totally likes you."

I knew she would do this, but I felt obligated to tell her something about yesterday.

It was not my place to mention Dean's dark, unknown secret and I wasn't about to bring up the encounter with Blake, so the invitation to the concert was my only option.

"No, he doesn't. We both agreed that we were going as friends," I replied, emphasizing on the word friends.

"Yeah after you suggested it!"

"We both were thinking it . . . I just turned out to be the one who said it aloud," I insisted, knowing I was pushing the believable boundaries.

Lucy clenched her jaw, and then sighed. "Riley, you're really bugging me. Just accept that he likes you and you like him! Stop pushing him and your feelings away."

"It's too soon . . ." I murmured, as we took our seats at our usual lunch table.

Truth of the matter was, I was scared. Of course, I could never tell Lucy this, but I wasn't ready for another relationship. I couldn't let someone close to me like that again. No way, not after Blake.

"No, it's not! If I had a hot, bad boy throwing himself at me, I'd take him in a heart beat," Lucy replied.

"If you haven't noticed, you and me are two completely different people," I snapped, my tone harsher than I intended.

But reality was, we couldn't be compared. Lucy, with her outgoing and bubbly personality, was more trusting and took one step at a time. I, on the other hand, had been emotionally and romantically scarred. I was afraid, guarded, and constantly concerned with the bigger picture.

Lucy took a brief moment of silence, letting my words linger in the air, before changing the topic.

"Have you thought of what you'll wear?" She asked, brushing my spiteful comment off.

"That's been the last thing on my mind," I muttered, more concerned with the recent, dramatic changes in my life.

"Well then, you leave me no choice. I'm coming over tomorrow and helping you get ready for the concert."

I sighed. "Fine, but nothing outrageous. I don't want to look like a different person."

"Deal." We shook hands, and then devoured our lunches.

After lunch, the rest of my day was completely normal. I went to my afternoon classes, rode home with Dean, and spent my Friday night expressing myself through my leather journal.

To most, an uneventful day would feel dry and dull. To me, it was a blessing. For the first time in months, I didn't have to worry about anyone. Not Blake, Dean, or anybody else for that matter. Just me, myself, and I.

My Saturday afternoon was relatively ordinary as well, until about four o'clock, when Lucy showed up to help me get ready.

"Are you excited?" Lucy asked, as she ran a brush through my hair.

"Yeah . . . I guess," I replied, shrugging my shoulders, with false nonchalance.

Up until now, I hadn't even thought about the concert. Now that Lucy was here, the nerves and anticipation were slowly suffocating me.

Lucy went to work; pulling out boxes, containers, compacts, brushes, tubes, bottles, pins, and cosmetics. As she did various things to my face and hair, I sat stiffly as I anxiously bounced my leg.

Really, I had no reason to be apprehensive; it was nothing more than a casual, friend outing. But there was something about it that made me feel queasy. I would be entering a foreign environment - one I certainly wouldn't fit into - with a guy who I had only hung out with on school days.

"Ready to see?" Lucy asked, after an hour filled with hard preparation.

"Sure, why not," I replied.

Lucy led me into the bathroom, where I faced the brightly illuminated mirror. But the girl staring back was not me. She was beautiful; with pin straight hair, dark rimmed eyes, and blood stained lips.

"What are you going to wear?" Lucy asked, leaning against the bathroom counter.

"I haven't decided," I said, still mesmerized by the reflection of that unfamiliar girl.

"I'll pick something out for you," she replied, with complete confidence.

I followed her out of the bathroom, and watched as she rummaged through my closet, destroying my organizational system. Moments later she came back with the dark wash jeans I had worn the day before and a basic black cotton v-neck shirt. Reaching into her backpack, she pulled out a black long-tie choker for my neck.

"What about a jacket? It's almost December, I'll freeze out there."

Lucy shrugged. "I guess you could wear your pea coat? Although it doesn't go with the rest of your outfit."

I sighed, knowing I looked like an asshole right now. Lucy had made me into a completely different person; something that I wasn't. Failure to find a matching jacket proved that my appearance was just a costume. This wasn't me, none of this was. Not my hair, not my makeup, and not my clothes.

"I know you worked really hard but . . ."

"You don't like it?" Lucy asked, obviously insulted.

"Who am I trying to fool? I'm not this edgy, sexy chick," I exclaimed, throwing my hands in the air. "I'm just a nerd!"

"Is that who you are? Is that who Riley Jennings really is? Or is that what people want her to be?"

My mouth hung open, but my brain drew a blank. Lucy had a point. Maybe I was still following what people typecasted me as. But I had been in that stereotype for so long, so I didn't know what else to be.

"I don't know who she is," I whispered, sulking in my chair.

Lucy placed a comforting hand on my shoulder, and said, "If you don't know, then what's the harm in trying? It might help you to step out of that label . . . along the way, you might discover who you really are."

Just then, we heard the doorbell echo through the house. My heart leaped, then filled with terror.

"He's here," I cried with panic. "What do I do? He's going to think I'm trying too hard." I suddenly became very uncomfortable in my outfit, wishing I had a skirt with ballet flats on instead. "He labels me just as much as everybody else does."

"Riley," Lucy curled her lips into a grin as she put her hands on my shoulders, "he's going to love it. You look so hot right now, he's not going to even care."

I pursed my lips together. "Really?"

"Yeah," she replied. "Now, go greet him. I'll go out the back door."

I gasped for some air, closed my eyes and started counting backwards from five. Opening them on one, I looked back at Lucy who gazed at me with comforting eyes.

"Thank you, Lucy . . ." I murmured.

She rolled her eyes. "What are friends for? Just make sure you give me all the details tomorrow."

Lucy packed up her bag while I rushed out of my room and headed for the stairs. I held onto the rail to steady myself as I made my way down. My stomach was churning from the nerves, and my legs felt like they would give out any minute now. Grabbing the front door handle, I opened the door.

"Hey," Dean cooed. The aroma of mint and strong cologne wafted through the doorway. He wore his usual attire of dark jeans, a dark t-shirt and a leather jacket. His hair was freshly combed and his chiseled face was smooth and clean shaven. "You look amazing."

"Really?" Nervously I tucked a lock of hair behind my ear. "Thanks."

"You're welcome," he said, with a beaming smile.

Slipping my arms into my coat that didn't match, I followed him out to the driveway. Parked behind Lucy's car was an unrecognizable black jeep wrangler.

"Where's your motorcycle?"

"I thought I'd bring a real car this time, to switch things up. Besides, it's getting too cold to drive around on my bike, especially at night," Dean answered, opening the passenger door for me.

"So have you ever heard of The Shins?" Dean asked, as he pulled the car out of my driveway.

"Yeah, I've heard of them . . . I don't really know any of their songs," I admitted.

"Well, lucky for you, we can listen to their CD," Dean said, pressing a button on the dashboard.

We listened to the first few songs in silence, soaking in the power of the music. The melodies were raw and catchy, the lyrics were fresh and clever, and the balance of the instruments was well done.

"Oh man, I love this song," Dean said, turning up the volume. "My band really wants to do a cover of this."

"You're in a band?" I yelled over the music. "I didn't know that."

"Yeah, we're not very good, but we're a band nonetheless."

Maybe the Black Knights were the name of his band, although I found that hardly reasonable. But I couldn't complain because I was already learning a little more about him, and that made me feel a bit better about all of the looming secrets surrounding our friendship.

After a decent twenty minute ride, Dean pulled into the parking lot for the concert venue. The building was shaped like an echoing dome, and music was already seeping through its walls. As we walked towards the entrance, we passed clusters of people who getting stoned or drunk before the concert. Dean protectively put his arm around me, and urged me to walk faster.

"It's disgusting how people can't have fun at a concert if they aren't sober," Dean whispered.

We made it the front, and Dean gave the usher our tickets. He was an elderly old man, with thick glasses that didn't fit his bumpy nose and what was left of his gray hair was combed over to the side.

"Not you again . . . " he growled, peering at Dean through his glasses. "I'm sorry, I don't think I can let you in. We don't want any of your shenanigans."

Dean nervously looked at me, then back at the man in the uniform. In a low voice, Dean murmured: "Look, that wasn't my fault."

"No, but you and your friends ruined the performance," the usher spat. I crinkled my eyebrows in curiosity as to what they were talking about.

"I'm not with them, am I?" He gestured towards me, as I stood there motionless with wide eyes. "It won't happen again."

"Fine." The usher ripped the tabs off the tickets then showed us to our seats in a middle row of the audience floor. Then he turned and pointed a bony finger at Dean. "No funny business," he hissed, before strutting away.

"What was that all about?" I asked, once the usher was out of sight.

"Nothing. Just forget about it," he said, shaking his head.

He obviously didn't want to talk about it and I didn't push it. So we changed the subject and talked carelessly until the show started.

"That was awesome," I raved once we were back at my house. The rush and adrenaline I got from the concert left me giddy. "They we're fantastic."

"I'm glad you had a good time," Dean replied. "We should do it again sometime."

"Definitely," I said, linking my arm with his without even thinking. But he didn't seem to think much of it. "Thanks again for taking me."

"Anytime," he murmured, as we reached my front door.

I paused for a moment, thinking about the last time we were standing at my front door. That was Thursday, when I learned that Dean was hiding a monumental secret from me.

The night, as incredible as it was, was almost over. I never wanted it to end, but if it had to, I wanted it to end on the highest note possible. The musical high had me floating on Cloud 9 and I didn't want a storm of dark secrets to rain down on me.

"Hey . . . I know you said you would tell me about the Black Knights tonight," I brought up, thinking about the earlier incident with the usher. "But . . . I'm in too good of a mood to talk about that right now. Maybe we can put that conversation off for another time."

I hadn't been this happy in a long time and I wanted to enjoy it for just a little bit longer.

"Riley, are you sure?" Dean asked, with dark brooding eyes. "Because we can talk about it if you want. A deal's a deal."

"No, it's okay," I whispered with a small smile. "Another time."

"Okay," he whispered back, giving me a warm smile back.

We stood there for a moment, silently communicating with our eyes. Sometimes his face was so handsome that it was hard to look at but right now, I couldn't take my eyes off him. Maybe it was the music that made me feel this way, maybe it was the second-hand marijuana smoke; who knows. All I knew was that I loved getting lost in his eyes.

Was he going to kiss me? I couldn't tell if I wanted him to or not.

I had been suffocating my attraction towards him since we first met, but at this very moment, they were trickling out. The feelings were there but so was the fear of getting hurt again.

"Goodnight Riley," he said, softly kissing my cheek.

With that, he skipped off, leaving me speechless, as the side of my face tingled with a hot, electrifying sensation.

CHAPTER 12

Monday morning marked the first day of December, also known as the day before my birthday. But that wasn't only the reason I loved the month of December.

No, I loved it because it was the last thirty-one days of the year, the beginning of the most beautiful season, winter, and the only month filled with true holiday cheer.

I spent the rest of my weekend trying to decipher the closing act of Saturday night. Endlessly, I tried to discover the meaning behind the kiss, as any teenage girl would. But as Lucy pointed out, a cheek peck could go both ways, as a friendly or romantic gesture. The only way to really determine what it symbolized was to see how the aftermath played out.

When Dean came to pick me up in the morning, I knew right away that things were different between us. For starters, he greeted me by wrapping his muscular arms around my torso, and running his cold fingers through my hair. Then, he kept saying over and over again how much fun he had, and how he loved hanging out with me.

I longed to read his mind, know what he was thinking. Undeniably, Saturday had sparked a change. But what was the change? What was he thinking, what was he feeling?

In this turmoil of unspoken emotions, I felt even more lost. Dean had proven himself trust worthy, reliable, and benevolent. But something still held me back. Somewhere, in the back of my head, a voice was saying history would repeat itself. It reminded me that in the beginning, Blake had given me no reason to believe he would cause any harm. It reminded me that Dean was still a mystery to me. It reminded me that for the sake of my mentality, I couldn't bear to go through the pain and suffering again.

And so, I wouldn't let myself. Rather than trying to read too much into Dean, I simply accepted what our current situation was; only a friendship and nothing more.

It was fifth period, when I was called down to the Guidance Office. As I walked through the lobby, I passed Blake and his father conversing with the school principal in low voices. As I strolled by, Blake's eyes were fixed on me, his glare burning down my core. My breathing quickened, as a sickening feeling formed in the pit of my stomach.

"Nice to see you again, Riley," Mrs. Delgado said, once I was seated in her office. I smiled meekly back at her, still disturbed and shaken up by the suspicious behavior I had just seen. "How's everything going?"

"Fine," I replied, knowing one word could not even begin to describe what was going on in my life right now.

"And the tutoring sessions?" She asked, peering over her reading glasses.

"Really well, I think," I said. "Like you said, he's really smart."

Mrs. Delgado pulled out a folder, and began flipping through the pages. "Well, you certainly are doing something right. Take a look," she said, handing me a document.

My eyes skimmed over Dean's progress report. He was pulling off B's in C's in all of his classes. Pride filled me up, as I smiled at the beaming grades. Seeing that certainly made my day better.

"That's fantastic," I exclaimed, handing the paper back to her.

"I don't know what you did, but you finally got him on track," Mrs. Delgado praised. "Keep up the good work with him."

After we shook hands, I left her office with a new bounce to my step. When I passed through the lobby again, only Blake remained. I hurried passed him, making sure to avoid any eye contact.

"Riley, wait," he called after me.

I gritted my teeth and stopped in my tracks. "What?"

"Look, I just want to talk to you," Blake replied.

"So talk," I sneered as my blood boiled. "Make it fast, I don't have all day."

He ran a hand through his messy, blond hair. "I miss you babe. I want you back. I can't sleep, I can't eat, I've been a wreck. I need you."

I scanned his blue eyes for sincerity, but all I saw was more lies. He hadn't changed a bit. His plea was just another phony, worked up act. This time I wouldn't fall for it.

"Well, you should have thought of that before you decided to abuse me," I spat.

"So I made a mistake, and hit you a few times," Blake said. "Doesn't everybody deserve a second chance? I'm giving you one!"

"A few times? I came home with bruises and cuts for months! I still have scars too. You lost your second chance a long time ago. I don't want your second chance either. I'd be an idiot if I ever got back together with you," I scoffed.

"Okay, fine," he said, rage filling inside of him. "If that's how you want it, then screw you. That's the last time I ever try being nice to you. And because you blew your second chance, you also blew your precious little bodyguard's chance too. We've got so much dirt on him, he'll be locked up for twenty years."

I was too mad to even question what he was talking about. I wasn't going to let myself listen to the lies Blake liked to spit out.

"Don't act like such a saint. You don't think I've got dirt on you? If you to do anything to Dean, I'll have you sent to jail for harassment, assault, and abuse," I snapped. Right now, as I saw it, two could play at this game.

"Good luck with that. If you haven't noticed, I'm gold, thanks to my father and the entire force that stands behind him. You can't touch this," Blake boasted.

"Tell that to the jury, asshole."

Blake grabbed me by the label on my blazer, pulling me closer to his crimson face.

"Watch what toes your stepping on. If you try anything funny, it'll be the last thing you do," Blake muttered, the words slicing like icy, cold blades. My confidence was shot, taking me from invincibility to vulnerability.

He let go, and stormed a few steps ahead. Then he stopped, turned around and said, "Oh and happy early birthday, you ungrateful bitch." He threw a small, clasped box onto the ground and walked away.

I bent down, and opened the satin, jewelry cube. Instead was a diamond pendant heart necklace. I admired the diamonds that reflected when they caught the light. Such a pity, I thought as I threw the present into the nearest trashcan.

After school, back at my house, I told Dean what happened.

"Why didn't you tell me your birthday was tomorrow?"

I rolled my eyes. "Dean, focus. That's not important. He's really serious about getting you in trouble."

"I've been getting in trouble all of my life, I'm not afraid of that. What I am afraid of is you trying to blackmail him for it, and getting your ass kicked for it," Dean replied.

"Well, that won't happen if you're around, right?"

Dean paused. "I don't know, Riley. Sick people like Blake always have a plan. What happens if he tries to hurt you and I'm not there? I'd love to be with you and protect you every minute of the day, but I can't."

"Do you really think he would go to extreme levels?"

"Other people have. Remember all those girls your dad told us about? The ones with abusive boyfriends who killed them because they sued?"

I gulped, reminded of those brutal stories. "Yeah, but maybe Blake wouldn't be like that."

Dean narrowed his deep eyes at me. "Maybe . . . but why take that chance?"

I sighed, discouraged by this whole situation. "It's just not fair. Why does he get away with it? Why doesn't he get punished?"

"He will. It might not be right away, but your dad is working really hard, and he's going to find a way to end all of this," Dean murmured.

"You think it will work? What if it's just a dead end?"

"I know it will. Your dad is a smart guy, and a great lawyer . . . there's always a loophole or a bluster and he'll find it."

I took a moment of silence, cursing the world for putting my father and me in this situation.

Because of his father, Blake got a get out of jail free card. Because of his father, Blake's chances of being convicted or arrested were slim to none. Because of his father, we were struggling and suffering to serve justice.

"So, tell me more about your birthday. You must be excited to turn seventeen," Dean said, trying to chance the topic and lighten the mood.

"Yeah, it's okay," I shrugged, "Just another year closer to my death."

"Well, that's kind of depressing," Dean replied, with a mocking tone.

"I just don't like birthdays, because they bring extra attention that I don't want. I don't see why we can't treat them like any other ordinary day."

Dean slightly nudged my arm. "I'm going to change your mind, and give you the best birthday ever."

"Good luck with that," I replied, rolling my eyes and secretly afraid of what he had in mind. "But you will fail."

"No, really. I'm going to take that as a challenge, and prove you wrong," Dean said, with a crooked, eager smile.

After we ate an afternoon snack, we started our homework. Occasionally, I would glance up from my textbook and watch Dean work. There was something so magnificent about him when he worked. His eyes were glued to the pages, his lips were curled in concentration, and he tugged at his messy, brown hair when he was stuck on a problem.

"So I heard that you're doing well in your classes," I remarked.

"Yeah?" He looked up from his notebook, his dark eyes glimmering. "I guess I have been doing better."

"Well, I'm proud of you."

"Thanks, Mom. Can we put my report card of the refrigerator?"

He laughed loudly at his joke, which only made me chuckle more. When our laughter died down, we went back to diligently working. Except now, I had broken his focus. Every time I snuck a peek at him, he caught me.

Charlie came home, grabbed a snack, awkwardly said hello, and ran up to his room. He obviously wasn't accustomed to having Dean around every day.

About an hour later, Dad came in. The three of us made small talk at first, then cut to the chase. After we explained what happened with Blake, my father's face curled with anxiety, as it always did. Sometimes, I didn't want to tell him, because it would only cause his distress to build. But he told me that every bit of information helps.

"Dean, if the Salatos try to get you legally involved or in any sort of trouble, I want you to come to me, and I'll represent you and be your attorney."

Dean nodded. "Yes sir."

My father turned to me. "Riley, if we're going to take legal action, we're going to need evidence. It's our word against the police force's word. We need proof."

"Dad, won't that be hard to find?"

"Yes, but it's our only shot," he muttered.

I pondered for a minute, recapping all of the interventions Blake and I had. Most of which were in private, and only seen by Dean.

"Dad, I have an idea . . ."

It was risky, but it was worth a try.

"What if . . . I provoked Blake enough to hit me in school, when nobody was around. Then, the video cameras would catch him in the act. I could go down to the security office, get the tape, and we would have video footage."

My father's mouth dropped open. I could tell that he wasn't sold on the idea. "Riley, I'm not going to let you put yourself in that kind of danger. No, absolutely not."

"Dad, please," I pleaded, knowing how successful this plan could be.

My father was speaking based on his paternal instincts rather than his attorney logic. As lawyer, he knew how useful that video could be in a court case. But as a father, he couldn't approve of allowing his own daughter to get hurt.

"Riley, my answer is no," he ordered firmly.

I pouted, and crossed my arms. He was being a good father, trying to protect his daughter, but this case was no longer about my safety; it was about bringing a criminal to light. I was torn. I wanted to rebel against my father, and do what I felt was best. But I also wanted to obey him, and respect his wishes.

The three of us sat in silence, unsure on how to proceed with the conversation. Dean must have felt the tension between my father and me, because he eventually changed the topic.

"Mr. Jennings, I was wondering if I could come over tomorrow and celebrate Riley's birthday?"

My father turned his head. "Riley wants to celebrate her birthday?"

"I don't, but he does," I muttered, with my arms still crossed.

"Well, I don't see the harm in a little birthday party," my father said, ignoring my comment. "Mom could make dinner, and I could run out and get presents."

Just the kind of attention I was hoping to avoid.

"Sounds like a plan," Dean said, shaking my father's hand.

When they finished devising my nightmare of a birthday, my father went upstairs to take a shower.

"You'll pay for this," I teased, as I walked Dean to the door.

"If you don't like it, then you can ruin my birthday, okay?" Dean pulled his arm through his leather jacket, as I nodded my head in agreement. "See you tomorrow, birthday girl."

CHAPTER 13

The blare of my alarm clock woke me up the next morning. Slamming my fist onto the robotic clock, I pulled the covers over my head. I wanted to stay in bed all morning, and hide from the world until this dreadful day passed.

Eventually, I forced myself up and out of bed. I went along with my usual morning routine, except occasionally, I had to stop what I was doing, answer the phone, and listen while a distant relative wished me a happy birthday. Dean arrived earlier than usual, so I had to take my morning bagel outside with me.

"Happy birthday to you . . . happy birthday to you . . . happy birthday, dear Riley, happy birthday to you . . ." Dean belted off key as soon as I walked outside.

I rolled my eyes, my skin crawling from the sound of that horrific song. It was embarrassing enough being put under the spotlight while people glorified an artificial day . . . but the corny song was the icing on the ostentatious birthday cake.

"Smile birthday girl," Dean cheered. "It's your special day."

"There's nothing special about it," I muttered, taking a bite out of my bagel.

"Somebody's grumpy," he said, pinching my cheek.

"I just don't want to deal with this," I gritted, as I climbed into the front seat of his jeep.

"You'll feel much better once you get your present," Dean replied, as he pulled onto the main road. "I spent all last night shopping for it."

"Really, you didn't have to do that. There's no need to waste your money."

"I didn't need to, but I wanted to," Dean replied. "There's a difference."

I leaned my head against the cool glass window, and muttered, "Suit yourself."

Throughout the school day, I tried my hardest to go unnoticed, and for the most part, I succeeded. One or two friends, who I hadn't talked to in months, came up to me and gave me warm, cheerful birthday wishes. I put on my best fake smile, thanked them, then went back to flying under the radar.

As any best friend would, Lucy knew about my unadulterated hatred for birthdays. She was the only person who did what I wanted; act as if my birthday was no different from any other regular day.

Overall, spending my birthday in school was not as painful as I predicted it to be. What was really going to be insufferable was celebrating it at home, with Dean and my family. The worst had yet to come. When the dismissal bell rung, I took my sweet time getting out to the junior parking lot. Undeniably, I was willing to do whatever it took to buy myself more time, and delay the dreadful celebration. Unfortunately, there was only so little I could do, and I eventually gave up.

"There you are," Dean exclaimed as I bitterly walked towards the car.

"Here I am," I scolded, crossing my arms around my chest.

Once we were on the road, Dean said, "So I have to stop by my house, and pick up your present. Mind if I drop you off at your house first?"

"Well, maybe I could come with you," I said, taking advantage of situation. "I'm in no rush to go home."

"No," Dean sternly replied. He quickly cleared his throat. "I need to wrap your present, and stuff . . ."

"Please?" I begged. "I really want to see your home."

"I don't know . . . I don't think it's a good idea," Dean murmured, suspiciously.

"Please, please, please?" I knew I was disregarding my manners, by inviting myself over and forcefully begging him, but desperate times called for desperate measures. Every day, I wanted to know more and more. Seeing his home would give me a raw glimpse into the part of his life I knew nothing about.

Dean briefly paused, tugging on his dark hair as he made a sharp turn. "Okay, fine, because it's your birthday, we can go to my house for a little bit."

"Thank you, thank you, thank you!" I exclaimed. Due to the circumstances, I didn't mind getting special treatment on my birthday. This was the only exception.

"You're welcome," Dean warmly replied. "But you have to promise that you won't complain when we go to your house."

I grunted a lousy, "Fine."

The drive to his house was longer than I expected. We drove on for miles, to the outskirts of town, and eventually, the area became foreign and unfamiliar to me. The houses were smaller, and the landscape and roads were shoddy. It felt like I was in a a completely different town.

Finally, Dean pulled up to a quaint, white cottage. His motorcycle was broadly parked in the driveway, and a miniature garden surrounded the mail box. Compared to the rest of the area, their property was actually very sweet. Hesitantly, I stepped out of the car, and followed Dean into his house. The inside of his house was not nearly as well kept as the outside. The walls were bare, painted in a mucky earth tone and mismatched furniture filled every room of the house.

"Wait here, while I wrap your presents," Dean ordered, before flying up the staircase.

Awkwardly, I stood alone, unsure of where to go. I drifted into his living room. The television set was propped up on the coffee table, which was placed just feet away from the worn fabric couch. Next to the couch were random sitting chairs, and lamp desk. As I decided against sitting, I drifted towards the mantle.

Baby pictures, cards, and other ornaments were sporadically placed along the cement block that hung above the fireplace. My eyes wandered, stopping on one individual photo. The dreary man in the frame was not Dean, though they shared similar features; dark, messy hair and intense eyes. Captured by the very essence of the old photograph, I picked the frame up, and tried to get a closer examination. A prayer in Ecclesiastical Latin was tucked into the corner of the frame. Intrigued, I began to try and translate it.

"What are you doing?" A deep, burly voice asked from behind me.

Caught off guard, I yelped. My hand lost grip of the picture frame, causing it to land on the floor with a clunk. As I caught my breath, I turned around to see another man.

He was younger than the man in the photograph, but older than Dean. He was shirtless, revealing rock solid abs and tattoos. His black eyes pierced at me, as he bent down to pick up the photo.

When he came back up, he shadily glared at me, and crossed his arms around his chest.

"Sorry," I stumbled, adverting his judgmental eyes. "I was just looking."

"Yeah, okay," he muttered. He walked passed me, leaving the scent of cigarettes, alcohol, and cologne behind him. "What are you doing in my house?"

"I'm . . . a friend of Dean's," I awkwardly replied.

"Oh. I usually know all of Dean's friends," he replied conde-scendingly. "I'm Alex, his brother."

"Nice to meet you," I stammered.

"Yeah . . ."

Alex sat there, quietly, his eyes slowly observing me. Then, he looked away, patted his thighs, and reached into his jean pocket. In his hand, he pulled out a Swiss army knife, which caused my eyes to widen in fear. Alex didn't pay notice to that, and went on to carve into a piece of wood.

As he worked, I stared, silently begging for Dean to come down and end this awkwardness.

"Are you going sit, or just stand there like an idiot?" Alex asked, his eyes still focused on the wood piece in his hand.

I gasped quietly, then hurried into a random chair. I sat stiffly, keeping my body tightly together. We sat in silence as the minutes went by, until Dean came down with a wrapped, rectangular box.

"Oh, great, you two met," Dean commented, as he reached the bottom step. I shot up, and walked towards him, standing by his side.

"Yeah, your new friend is . . . interesting," Alex remarked, waving his knife in my direction. Dean glared intensely at his brother. "Tell Mom when she gets home that I'm out with a friend, will you?"

"Should I tell her who? Or just let her assume who it is?" Alex asked, with a jocular tone in his voice, which caused my eyebrows to raise in interest of what he was referring to. Alex was silent. "Whatever," Dean replied, his voice filled with aggravation. "I'll see you later."

"No, you won't, I'll be out with the guys," Alex spat. "You're more than welcome to join us. It's been a while."

"I'm good," Dean replied, sneaking a peek at me.

I tried my best to not react, but I couldn't help but wonder if he was referring to the Black Knights. In this moment, I silently scorned myself for not having the conversation about the mysterious group this past Saturday. Soon, I kept reminding myself. I would know soon.

"Your loss," Alex mumbled.

Dean eagerly rushed me out the door before I could even say good bye to Alex. Not that it mattered anyway; he was rather unpleasant.

"Sorry you had to deal with that. Alex can be an arrogant asshole sometimes," Dean said, once we were on the road again.

I nodded my head in agreement. "You got that right."

We left the conversation at that. There were was so much I wanted to ask about; what their banter was about, who the man in the photo was, and where his parents were. But I restrained myself. I had gotten what I wanted, at Dean's disdain. I knew better than to push the envelope any further. My questions, my curiosity would have to wait until another day.

The celebration had already begun back at my house. Balloons, decorations, and presents were already lavishly spread around the house. Before I partook in this dreadful arrangement, I excused myself to the bathroom, took three Advil tablets, and mentally prepared myself for the torture I would soon endure.

When I got back downstairs, the boys were conversing naturally in the living room, while my mother cooked in the kitchen.

"So who's your friend?" My mother asked with a displeased tone. She chopped away at an onion, taking her anger out on the vegetable.

"Just a guy from school."

"Interesting. I didn't know your school accepted deviants now . . . or that my very own daughter would befriend one of them."

"Mom, would it kill you to be open minded once in your life? Get to know him first, before you judge him," I spat, irritated by her natural instinct. Just because I knew she would react this way didn't mean it still didn't piss me off.

"I don't need to know him . . . I can tell right away, just how he looks," she replied. "I mean look at the guy: tattoos, leather jacket, combat boots, I've seen it all before. He's no different from any other troublemaker out there. Why didn't you invite Blake? He's a much more respectable, young man."

I couldn't help but get a little mad at her ignorance.

"We broke up but of course, you don't care enough about my life to know anything about it," I hissed, before turning on my heel. I left my mother in the kitchen, and joined the men in the living room.

Charlie was admiring each of Dean's tattoos. Finally, my little brother was warming up to him. Dean smiled at Charlie, then at me, as I sat down next to him on the couch.

"Dad, can I get one?" Charlie asked with sheer excitement.

"When you're older," my father replied half-listening, as he flipped the page of his evening newspaper.

After a few more minutes of bonding and playing with Athena, my mother called us in for dinner. Salad, vegetables, chicken cutlets, and gravy were spread across the table. My father made a toast, honoring my birth and claiming that I'm the best daughter he could ever have, which only made me feel embarrassed and antsy.

"This is delicious, Mrs. Jennings," Dean politely said, trying to win her over.

"Thanks," she replied, tonelessly. I cleared my throat, and scowled at her. She pursed her lips. "So Dean, tell me about yourself. What do you like to do?"

"Well . . . I like music," Dean answered, obviously put on the spot.

"Oh, well that's nice," my mother replied in her cheerful, fake tone. "Any ideas where you want to go to college?"

"No," he instantly replied. My mother smirked, causing him to cover his answer up more. "I mean . . . I haven't given it much thought yet. Right now, I'm focused on getting my grades up."

"Oh." In that one word, I could tell that she was judging him to the fullest degree, convinced that her first impression was correct.

"Dean's actually really smart," I blurted out, trying to defend him.

"I'm sure he is, Riley," my mother said, as if he wasn't there. Dean glanced at me, uncomfortable by the situation.

After we all finished, and cleared out plates, my mother brought out the birthday cake. Seventeen candles were lit, illuminating words that said HAPPY BIRTHDAY RILEY in frosting. As they sang to me, I felt my cheeks redden, waiting for this moment to pass. When it came time to blow out my candles, I froze. Eight eyes stared at me, waiting for me to put the room in darkness. I stood stiffly, watching the flames flicker and the wax melt, unsure of what I wanted.

A wish should not be made on the spot, nor granted because it's somebody's birthday. If I'm going to make a wish, it's because

I want something so badly in that very moment, not because it's a birthday tradition to ask and receive. So I blew out the candles with a blank mind.

After we finished eating the cake, it was present time. My father went up to his office, and brought down his digital camera, so he could capture each moment.

As I opened my presents, I deliberately avoided making eye contact with the large lens pointed in my face. My first gift was from Charlie. Inside the small, cardboard box held a suede bracelet. Then, I opened my parents' gift, which was the Amazon Kindle.

"Now you won't have to deal with those heavy books that you like to carry around and read," my father teased.

"Thanks Dad, its great!"

Then, I opened the present from Dean. As I ripped away the birthday wrapping paper, I felt eager to see what was inside. I slid off the top, and unfolded the tissue paper. A studded leather jacket with silver zippers was neatly folded inside. Vaguely, I heard my mother scoff at his present, but I didn't care what she thought.

"Wow," I whispered, running my fingers across the metal studs.

"You like it?"

"I love it," I replied, staring him in the eyes.

As he looked back at me, I almost forgot that my family was still in the room with us. Bringing the jacket up to my chest, I gave it a big squeeze. The leather felt soft and cool against my burning hot skin.

My mother spent the rest of the evening in the kitchen, claiming she was cleaning. But after an hour, I knew she was just purposely ignoring Dean. I had no complaints, though. I didn't want her around, victimizing Dean. Charlie, Dean, Dad and I were perfectly fine without her pestering company.

"Well, I should probably go, it's getting late," Dean said, standing up from the couch and ending the conversation.

"Here, I'll walk you to your car," I offered.

Dean slipped on his leather jacket, and for the first time, I put on mine. Instantly, the power of the jacket filled me up and made me feel like a brand new person. We embraced the cold winter wind, and walked towards his car parked in the driveway.

"Sorry about my mom," I apologized for her rude actions.

"It's okay, my brother is just as bad," Dean replied, shaking his head. "But over all, good birthday?"

"Not terrible," I lied. Admittedly, Dean had made this particular birthday way better than any other I could think of.

"You know you liked it," he said, with a cheeky grin.

I blushed slightly, and couldn't hide my budding smile. "Okay, maybe I did, slightly."

"That's more like it," Dean whispered.

Suddenly, he pulled me in for a tight bear hug. As he broke away, I thought he was going to get in his car, and drive way.

Boy, was I wrong.

Dean lingered, his face ever so close to mine. Putting his hands in my hair, he pulled me in and pressed his soft, warm lips into mine, causing my knees to tremble. But I didn't push him away, I didn't even want him to stop. If I could back and blow out my candles again, I would wish for this moment to never end. I wanted to stay in his arms, feeling his lips on mine, forever.

My regrets, my confusion, my paranoia all flew out the window. I didn't care anymore about getting hurt, or it being too soon. I wanted him, and that, I was finally sure of.

CHAPTER 14

After we broke apart, Dean left, without an explanation or a clarification. In that giddy, high moment, I didn't need one. It was only until later that night, when I was lying wide awake in my bed, that I craved some sort of answer. Sure enough, he kissed me. But what did that mean? What did that say about our friendship?

Now, we were stranded in the middle of vast abyss of unspoken terms and misplaced labels. I was swimming in a pool of uncertainty. I didn't have a clue to why he kissed me or what it symbolized. He could have kissed me on pure impulse, or he could have been planning it all along.

It was only when my eyes began to close that I realized there wasn't anything I could do about it now. All of this would have to wait until tomorrow.

Tomorrow came, but Dean did not.

Dean, who was always prompt, never showed up. I stood in the freezing cold for fifteen minutes, looking up and down the street, waiting for him to arrive . . . but he never did.

When the bus came, I had no choice but to take it. This time around, I was too angry to even acknowledge the rowdy kids I had to share the bus with. Fuming with rage, I detested him for making me look and feel like an idiot. He could have called, could have told me that he wasn't going to school, could have explained everything before he left so I wouldn't have to spend all day and all night worrying about us.

He could have, but he didn't.

If it had been any other day, I wouldn't have cared as much. But after what happened and how we left things, I needed to see him, just so my mind could be put at ease. Was he aware of the insanity he was putting me through? Was he feeling just as confused as I was? Probably not, or else he wouldn't have decided to skip school.

I walked into Chemistry, almost expecting to see him sitting at his desk. But his desk was empty.

"Lawrence?"

"Here."

"Lepol?"

"Here."

"Marks?"

Silence.

Dean was not there to answer his name. Dean was not there to be marked present on the attendance sheet. Dean was not there.

We took a test, one that I thought I was prepared for. But every question seemed to baffle me, and I couldn't find it in my right mind to focus. Every few minutes, I would subconsciously glance at the door, hoping Dean would bust through in the middle of class. But he never did.

I was being over-dramatic and needy, but I couldn't help it. I was going mad, eager to see his comforting smile, desperate to hear his deep voice tell me everything was okay. Where was he? What was so important that he felt the need to skip school?

As soon as the bell rang, I rushed towards the door. I needed to get out of that classroom.

"Riley," Lucy called after me. "Riley!" I slowed down as she sped up. "What's going on with you?"

"What are you talking about?"

"You were acting strange all period . . . you were one of the last people to hand in your test, when usually you're the first. And the only time you looked up from your test was to look at the door."

"Sorry."

"Where's Dean?"

"Wish I knew," I lowly replied.

She grunted. "Well, how was your birthday dinner?"

"Why are you asking so many questions? Stop prying, would you?" I snapped, without justification. She looked hurt, so I drew back. "Sorry, I'm just in a really bad mood."

Lucy raised her eyebrows at me, so I continued: "Dean kissed me last night . . . but now I'm so confused about us, and I've been so eager to talk to him, but I can't do that now, because he's not here."

"Riley, relax. Don't worry too much. He obviously likes you, and he kissed you."

"I know . . . I wish I could just be happy and go with the flow, but I need some sort of explanation. I have no idea what he wants, how he feels, or anything!"

"You know what?" Lucy pondered. "You're not nervous because you don't know how he feels . . . you're nervous because you don't know how you feel."

Lucy had just struck a chord within me. I was taken back by her inflection. "What do you mean?"

"Well, you admit you have feelings for him now, right?"

"Yeah . . . I think so. I don't know though. I mean I guess. I can't deny that I don't feel anything towards him because of course I do."

"But you're still afraid, aren't you?"

I took a moment, thinking about it. Blake traumatized me. My first relationship was a worse case scenario. After suffering with such abuse, jumping into a new relationship and becoming vulnerable again seemed almost suicidal. It was unrealistic to think that I would ever be in any mental state to start over.

The wounds may heal, but the scars never do. That little voice inside my head would never disappear.

"Yeah," I mumbled, nodding my head. "I'm scared to death."

"So your fear is making you paranoid about everything," Lucy concluded.

I bit my bottom lip. "I guess so. Maybe it's too soon.

"Maybe it is, and maybe it isn't. Just don't rush or jump to any conclusions. Give yourself time and don't let it mess with your head," she advised softly. She looked deeply into my eyes and then pulled me in for a soft hug.

I tried to follow her guidance for the rest of the day, but it was easier said than done. My mind would race at a million miles per hour, as each thought lead to another. It was uncontrollable and sickening. Literally, I felt like I was going insane.

Surprisingly, it was more maddening at home. Nothing could distract me. I tried writing in my journal, listening to music, doing my homework, watching the television, but somehow it all brought me back to Dean.

Halfway through the night, I gave up, and chose to lie perfectly still in my bed with my eyes open, glued to the white bare ceiling above me. I stayed in the same position as the hours passed by, and the night crawled on.

It was two in the morning when I finally budged. The repetitive, continuous pelting at my bedroom window finally began to irritate me. As I opened my window to investigate, I saw him, standing with a handful of pebbles.

"Come down," I heard him say.

I rubbed my eyes a few times, assuming that I was imagining things. But he was still there, beaming brightly up at me, his face illuminated by the glow of the moon.

"What are you doing here?"

"Just please come down."

I didn't protest. I didn't yell at him for putting me through hell, reject him because I was angry, or ignore him because I was upset.

No, I simply crawled out my window in my pajamas and sweater, held onto the ledge, and climbed my way down the side of the house. When it was time to let go, I jumped, and landed safely in Dean's strong arms. As I looked up at him, his face so close to mine, I noticed new, fresh scratches and wounds. When I was about to ask, he released me, and stormed forward, turning at the corner of my street.

"Dean, wait up," I called after him, picking up my speed. "Where are you going?"

"We are going out for a bit."

"Are you nuts?" I objected, still catching my breath. I rubbed my arms to create heat friction, and regretted not bringing a heavier jacket. "In case you haven't noticed, it's two in the morning!"

"All the more reason to go out," he replied as he straddled his bike. "It's such a lovely hour, don't you think?"

There was no denying that he was acting differently. In fact, he was acting like a complete lunatic.

But why? Maybe he was as confused as I was and just handled it differently.

"Well, are you coming?" Dean waved the lacquer helmet in front of me.

The sparkle in his dark eyes told me I had no choice but to take the helmet and join him on the bike. The engine came to life with a roar, and we were off, zooming down the quiet, dark streets of town. The bitter winter night air and the lack of sufficient clothing caused me to pull myself closer to Dean's body warmth. After cruising around for a bit, Dean stopped and parked us next to the Saugatuck river creek.

We sat by the body of water, admiring the moonlight that reflected off the rippling current. By that point, I was shivering from the cold, so Dean draped his leather jacket over my shoulders.

"Where were you today?" I finally asked.

"Just needed a personal day," he dimly replied, breaking a twig with his hands.

"Are these from today?" I reached up, lightly touching his bruised face. "Is this why you missed school?"

Dean shooed my hand away, but said nothing. I could tell that he was upset, distraught, even embarrassed, so I moved on.

"About yesterday . . ."

"I'm really sorry, Riley. I shouldn't have done that. I know it was too soon for you."

"Don't apologize," I stammered, fearing the point he was about to make.

"No, I have to. It wasn't right. I wasn't being considerate of how it might have affected you, especially after all you went through with Blake."

"Dean, it's not like that," I insisted.

"Riley, you don't have to try and make me feel better. I like you, I do, but I think it would be better if we just stay friends."

Suddenly, the cold didn't bother me anymore. I could hear my heart beat thumping loudly in my ears. How could I be so stupid, so foolish? Why did I let my guard down, only to be hurt? His words echoed in my head, cutting me again and again like icy cold razor blades

I knew it was too good to be true, I knew it wasn't meant to be. And yet, I pushed my reasonable doubts aside, and set myself up for this. No wonder I was so paranoid . . . it was my subconscious mind telling me that this wasn't right, that heartbreak was right around the corner.

"Are you okay?"

"I'm fine," I gritted through my teeth as I removed his jacket from my shoulders. "I'm just tired. Can we go home now?"

Dean took me directly home. I wanted to be mad at him, I really did, but I couldn't blame him. It was my own damn fault, for always being so stupid and letting any justified inhibitions I had go straight out the window.

Would I ever learn?

When he pulled up to my driveway, I got off, and handed him the helmet. Before walking up my lawn, I took one look back at him. Then, the unstoppable word vomit came.

"You know what? I'm actually not okay," I screeched, staring him dead in the eye.

"What?"

"I'm not okay. I'm really hurt. You know, I really like you too, and maybe for a moment, I thought we could be something more, but I see now that I was wrong. I spent all night and all day thinking and worrying about you, and me, and us. Now, I just feel like an idiot for even wasting my time."

"I'm not good enough for you. You deserve someone better. I mean, take a look at yourself, and the bright future you have . . . and look at me," he whispered. "Riley, I'm not worth it."

"But you are."

Dean dolefully shook his head. "No, I'm really not. I'm not going to let you throw your life away with some guy like me."

"I'm not asking for a life long commitment," I murmured, narrowing my eyes down at him.

"But I am, because you're the type of girl who deserves it," he murmured. "And I can't give that to you. Look, it's just easier, for the both of us, if we just stay friends."

"Friends . . ." I repeated, letting the term soak through my skin, and cut through my veins. In the beginning, I always intended on always being just friends. I had forced myself for weeks to only want that. Now, friends was the last thing I wanted to be.

"Yeah, we can still do that, right?"

"Sure."

I was hurt. Not by him, but by myself. Maybe after months of being hurt by someone else, I had turned into masochist. I felt as though I went out of my way to seek pain. I shouldn't have given the kiss a second thought. I silently cursed myself for putting myself through hell all day trying to decipher and extract meaning from it.

The sad truth was I think I was so eager to find long term happiness. Dean had given me the moon, but I wanted more. I was a fool to think Dean could give me unlimited happiness. No, that was something that only I could give myself.

"I'm not," I coldly replied. "Goodnight Dean."

I didn't hear Dean's engine start until I was safely back in my room. As soon as I knew he was gone, I cried until the pain numbed and the morning came.

CHAPTER 15

The next morning, I was a mess. It was the second time this week that I didn't want to go to school. But unlike my birthday, I was avoiding one person in particular rather than hiding from everyone.

I hated myself. I had lost all sensibility, lit myself on fire, and watched as I burst into flames. From the beginning, I knew Dean wasn't an option.

Why, after all I had been through, did I jump on the chance to be with the first man who ever treated me with a little decency?

I skipped my shower, threw on a baggy sweatshirt, and tied my knotted hair into a messy ponytail. My stomach refused my morning bagel, so I went outside, and sat on the stoop while I waited for the bus. But to my surprise, Dean pulled up on his motorcycle.

"Hey," Dean mumbled with dark, sorrow filled eyes. "Hope you don't mind that I brought the bike."

"Nope," I sharply replied, as I strapped the helmet onto my throbbing head.

I climbed onto the seat, hanging as far back as possible. I couldn't bring myself to wrap my arms around his waist. The engine came to life, humming as it sat in neutral.

"Riley, I need you to hold on."

I scowled, and inched forward, digging my fingers into his sides. Dean didn't push for more, so he took off. As soon as we got to school, I rushed inside before Dean got the chance to restart the conversation.

I looked back once, just to see Dean glumly lingering behind, with his hands stuffed deeply in his dark jeans. He looked guilty, and I knew that he was blaming himself for what happened. Dean didn't deserve this because it wasn't his fault, but I wanted him to feel the pain I was feeling. It wasn't right . . . scratch that, it was cruel, but I needed to know that I wasn't the only one suffering in this world.

As the day went on, the suffering got worse.

Mr. Richards started chemistry class by handing back our graded tests from yesterday. When Mr. Richards came by Dean's desk, he told him to see him after class so he could make up the exam. My day went from bad to awful in just a few seconds. On top of my exam, next to my name, was my first D- in crimson red ink.

"Come see me after class," Mr. Richards mumbled before moving on.

The rest of the class was a complete blur.

The bell finally rang, and within moments, it was just Mr. Richards, Dean, and me. Dean lingered at his desk, letting me go up first. I made the walk of shame up to my teacher's desk, clutching my failure tightly in my hand.

"Riley, I don't know what happened," Mr. Richards said sympathetically. "You're one of my best students, so I'm surprised. Did you not understand the material?"

"I thought I did . . ."

"I see, well did you sleep poorly the night before? Were you distracted by something?" His persistent questions were not something I was willing to answer, so I grumbled in response. "Is everything okay?"

"Everything's fine," I quickly replied, avoiding his inquisitive eyes. I resisted the urge to look back at Dean.

Everything was fine. I wasn't being abused anymore, I wasn't dying, I wasn't living on the street and selling my body for money.

For once, I was living like an average teenager, facing average teenage problems. Surprisingly, teenage drama affected me much more than any of the other shit I had to go through. Strange how rejection from a crush destroyed me inside, but abuse from a boyfriend only fazed me.

"Are you sure? You haven't been acting like yourself."

"What makes you say that?" I snapped, cocking my head to the side.

"Well, you just seem different," he muttered, scanning my messy ensemble.

Of course . . . if preppy, little Miss Jennings isn't wearing a skirt and blouse, then something must be wrong. If star student, soon-to-be valedictorian Riley gets one bad grade, she must be going through a rough time.

"I'm fine, everything's fine," I gritted. "Thanks . . ."

With that, I stormed out of the room with no acknowledgement to Dean behind me.

I felt myself crack, as I crumpled up my test and threw it away in the trashcan near the door.

The halls swarmed with students scrambling to get to class. I felt their eyes silently judging me as they passed by. These people don't know me. They don't know who I am, or what I've been through. They didn't know then, and they don't know now.

The bell rang, and suddenly I was alone with nowhere to go. My hands tingled, begging for redemption. My feet led me astray, searching for my destiny.

On the move, with everything spinning around me, I crashed into someone.

"Hey, watch it," I sneered as if it was their fault. I dropped to my knees and began to collect my dropped belongings.

"Riley?"

It could only be fate that would lead me to Blake. We were the only people in sight, alone but protected by the walls of the school. The world had given me this opportunity, and wanted me to take it.

Everything instantly turned crystal clear, and I knew exactly what I had to do.

"Here, let me help you with that," Blake kindly offered, as he crouched down beside me and gathered my books.

"I don't need your help," I spat, snatching my stuff from his grasp.

"So you'll take Dean's help, but you won't take mine."

My cheeks burned at the sound of his name. But I didn't let that distract me from my goal.

"Dean's a good guy . . ." I swallowed hard from the guilt. "And you're just a piece of shit. Why should I take your help?"

"Because you had a relationship with this piece of shit for six months."

"And it was the worst six months of my life," I spat.

"Well, it was the best six months of mine . . ." Then something happened in that moment, something that had never happened before.

For the first time, I actually saw guilt, vulnerability, and remorse in Blake's eyes. I tore myself away. The roles had flipped. Now, I was the one causing the pain between us. I was about to hurt him, scar him, ruin his life, just as he did to me. It killed me that I was the villain, the monster, but it had to be done.

"Well, you had a funny way of showing it..." I murmured, digging the knife into his gut even further.

"So I'm not perfect but that doesn't mean --"

I cut him off. "Not perfect? You're the farthest thing from it!"

"God, could you let me finish?" His eyes blared with fire. Now, we were getting somewhere.

Come on, Riley, I told myself. Keep going.

"There's no point. You've got nothing important to say," I replied. "Everything you say is a lie."

"How can you say that? I'm not lying when I say that you mean the world to me."

"Bullshit," I muttered, rolling my eyes for emphasis.

"You think I'm lying?"

"I know you are . . . your actions speak for themselves."

Jackpot.

Blake forcefully pushed me into a secluded corner, closed off by the lockers, then pressed his body close to mine.

"What are they saying now?" Blake asked, before sucking on my neck. "That I love you and want to please you?"

"Get your hands off me," I protested, pushing him away. But he came right back, like a rubber band.

"Stand still," he demanded, as his hand reached up to grope my breast. "God, it's been forever."

"Get off!"

From there, everything played out perfectly, as if it was in slow motion. His hand covered my mouth to muffle out my screams.

He touched me wherever and however he pleased despite my resistance. But out of the corner of my teary eye, I caught a glimpse of the school video camera hanging in the high right corner, catching our every move. And suddenly, the pain wasn't so bad.

When the deed was done, and he was gone, I pulled myself up from the cold floor and washed up in the closest bathroom.

Stage one was complete.

As I tended to my face, the bite marks, and the scratches, I thought of my father's wishes. This was the first time I disobeyed him. He had my best interest at heart, but I knew that I needed to do this. It was our only shot. If we didn't have this evidence, we had no chance in court.

"Hey Jimmy." I peeked into the computer lab where super techie Jimmy Yeens was fiddling with some wires. "Can you get me into the security room?"

"No can do, Riley," he replied, his eyes focused on two colored cables. "Only authorized personnel."

"Come on, Jimmy, please? For me?"

He looked up from his work, and glanced at me through his thick framed glasses. "What's in it for me?"

"I'll do all of your Calculus homework for a week," I reasoned.

"Make it a month," he demanded, standing up and brushing off his black cargo pants. "And you've got yourself a deal."

I grunted. "Fine. Let's go."

I followed Jimmy out of the computer lab, through the empty hallways, up to the exclusive dark door. Jimmy pulled out a ring, fumbled with each key until he found the right one. The door swung open, and we entered the darkly lit room. Mini screens were illuminated by the footage of every quarter in school.

"Thanks Jimmy, I can take it from here," I said, tearing my eyes away from the main lobby security camera.

"Don't worry about it. If anybody asks, I didn't bring you here."

After he left, I started my search. I rewound each security tape, and closely watched for Blake in the act. As I watched, I was surprised to see what some people did when they thought nobody's watching. But I didn't need blackmail, I needed proof.

I finally found it. Despite the black and white resolution, Blake was easy to identify. It hurt to watch myself getting sexually assaulted, as if I re-lived it all over again. I ejected the tape, then tucked it under my sweatshirt.

Just as I was clearing out and covering up my track, the door swung open, letting in the fluorescent light from the hallway.

"Miss. Jennings, what do you think you're doing?"

Principal Werner peered down at me, crossing his arms in front of him. Behind him stood the school security guard, who held Jimmy by his shirt. My heart dropped into my stomach. This was not going to be pretty.

"I...um...was..." I stumbled over my words. I really need to learn how to lie . . .

"I think you better come with me," Mr. Werner scorned sternly. "My office."

Now, I had really done it . . .

CHAPTER 16

Destiny had just slapped me in the face.

I had done everything right, as I obediently followed the path it paved for me, only to end up here. Never in my life had I ever been sent to the principal's office. Never in my life had I ever gotten in trouble.

I guess there's a first time for everything.

The sacred security video tape began to slip from the hold of my sweatshirt. I couldn't let Principal Werner take the tape away from me. I couldn't let him watch it. This matter was to be handled by the high court of law, not by the school. The administration at Oxford High could not replace an honorable judge and his righteous jurors. It wouldn't be lawful, and it couldn't be substituted. If Principal Werner got his hands on that tape, the case would automatically fall into his hands. I couldn't let that happen.

Keeping my head bent low, I discreetly tucked the tape into the waistband of my jeans.

"Keep walking, Miss Jennings," Principal Werner urged, as I tried to picked up the pace.

After a walk that seemed to go on forever, we reached the main office. Jimmy and I were thrown into principal's private office, where we anticipated our doom.

"Jimmy, what the hell did you do?" I sneered, as soon as Principal Werner left us for a brief moment.

"What did I do?" Jimmy retorted, leaning over the arm of his chair. "I didn't do anything wrong. This is your fault!"

"It's not my fault you got caught by the security guard!"

"Enough!" Principal Werner boomed as he entered his office. Jimmy and I both slumped back in our chairs as the principal took his seat behind the large oak desk that glared at us. "I am extremely disappointed and disgusted by both of your behavior. Two of the brightest students in school are sitting in my office. Think of the example you two are setting for the rest of the student body."

"Sir . . . I don't think I deserve to be here. This is Riley's fault, not mine. I didn't break any rules," Jimmy said, throwing me under the bus.

"Mr. Yeens, when you were appointed student technician, you took an oath. By allowing an unaccredited student to enter a restricted area on your behalf, you broke that oath. For that, you will have one week of lunch detention, as well as be reviewed by the administration, who will reconsider your initiation as student technician," Principal Werner informed, causing Jimmy to groan loudly. "However, you are correct. The issue rests with Miss Jennings here, not you. So you may leave."

Jimmy, who obviously was alarmed by the situation, quickly grabbed his backpack and left the room. Principal Werner took a moment to glower at me, his eyes burning with displeasure.

"Miss Jennings, I can't help but admit that I'm utterly surprised by this."

"You aren't the first one to be . . ." I muttered under my breath, referring to Mr. Richards.

"What was that?" Principal Werner asked, even though I knew he heard me loud and clear.

I shook my head. "Nothing."

"Right. Anyway, I can't seem to wrap my head around this. Miss Jennings, you have perfect attendance, stellar grades, and a clean record. Breaking into the security room and tampering with school property just doesn't sound like something you would do."

Of course not. Because for twelve school years, I've been Riley fucking Jennings.

As the entire public school system sees it, Riley Jennings can't do anything wrong, because she's perfect! She's the golden child. She would never break a school rule, get a bad grade, or disobey her parents. Well, Riley Jennings is sick and tired of it. She's sick and tired of doing what everybody wants her to do. She's exhausted from trying to be the best, trying to fit into her perfect stereotype. Her frustration has continued to build, until now, where she wants to be her.

I'm Riley Jennings, but not the Riley Jennings people want me to be. I want to be the real me for once.

"Your parents are on their way. They should be here any minute now. Then, we can all discuss this. Until then, I would you like to sit here, and think about what you've done."

Principal Werner left me to my solemn silence. But thinking was the last thing I wanted to do. I didn't want to think anymore, I wanted to act.

I avoided thinking at all cost. I distracted myself, observing all of the mesmerizing objects that decorated the room; the diplomas that hung on the wall, the large globe that was in the corner, the gold pleated books that were placed in the bookshelf, and the portraits of past principals. It was enough to occupy my time until my parents arrived.

When they did, all hell broke lose. As my mother went on a rampage, and my father silently brooded, I tuned it all out. My focus was on the video tape that was still in my possession. My father wouldn't understand, and my mother wouldn't know, but I was satisfied with my decision and didn't regret a thing. Sure, I had gone through pain and punishment to get there, but it would count in the long run, and that made it worth it.

"Are you sure there is nothing we can do?" My mother's voice pierced through the cold, crisp air as I finally started to listen.

"I'm afraid not. We have a very strict policy, and we make no exceptions. Tampering with school property and violating unauthorized areas earns a student three days of suspension."

"Will this go on her permanent record?"

"Yes ma'am, but with a relatively clean transcript, like your daughter's, most colleges will overlook it," Principal Werner explained.

"Well that's a relief," my mother replied, as if it would affect her chances of getting into the "perfect Ivy League."

"Miss Jennings," Principal Werner turned his attention to me, "consider yourself lucky and on probation. If you cause any more trouble, the severity of this issue will reach great heights. Don't let it."

I nodded dolefully, and followed my parents as we got up to leave the room.

"Just a second," Principal Werner interjected. "If you two don't mind, I'd like to have another word with Riley alone."

My parents nodded and exited his office. Principal Werner waved to the chair for me to take a seat again. He rested on the edge of his desk, a mere couple of feet away from me.

"Now that that's taken care of, let's get down to it," he said. "I know you, Riley. You're a smart girl. A young woman such as yourself doesn't just break into a security footage room for fun. You had a reason and an important one at that."

I raised my eyebrow at him and sat up a little, surprised by his on-target inflection.

"I know you snatched one of the security tapes," he leaned a bit closer and raised his eyebrow. "I saw it peaking out while we were walking."

I slouched back down, absolutely defeated. The gig was up and I was back at square one.

Devastated, I reached under my sweatshirt, pulled the tape out and extended it to him.

He waved his hand. "Riley, I'm not going to ask for it back." He lowered his voice and spoke in a soft tone. "Whatever it is, it must be important. Far be it for me to keep it from you."

My eyes widened. Was this really happening?

He reached out and put a hand on my shoulder. Normally, people would freak at the thought of a school official touching a student but this was different. He touched me lightly, in a comforting but concerned manner.

"Use it well," he said, peering over his glasses.

I bit down on my bottom lip, trying to force back the tears of relief. "Thank you, Principal. You have no idea how much that means to me."

He gave my shoulder a squeeze, then let go. Buttoning up his blazer, he made his way the chair behind his desk.

"That will be all," he proclaimed.

I took a deep breath, gave him a nod and made my way to the door.

As I reached out for the door knob, he said: "Oh and Riley, try not to tell the other students that I let you have this . . . only the good kids get special treatment."

I closed my eyes and smiled a little. "Of course, Principal Werner. My lips are sealed."

"Good," he said, rolling up the sleeves of his blazer before pulling out a notebook. "See you in three days!"

Closing the doors behind me, I tucked the video into the waistband of my jeans again. I leaned against the wall and had myself a little laugh of relief. No matter how mad my parents were, no matter how much school suspension sucked, I was overjoyed.

Despite how happy I felt on the inside, I kept my attitude on the outside quiet and remorseful. I made no attempts to speak to my parents the entire ride home, not because I felt shame but because I just didn't really want to hear whatever they had to say. In this situation, I couldn't explain myself to a point where we would understand. So it was just better to stay silent.

It was going pretty well, until my mother finally spoke up halfway through the car ride.

"Riley, what were you thinking? What exactly was so important that you needed from the security office?"

"Nothing, Mom. Don't worry about it," I mumbled, trying to prevent the conversation from continuing.

"Don't worry about it? Riley, you were just suspended and you tell me to not worry about it? Do you even care? Do you even care that your future is slipping between your fingers?"

"Nope."

That was the truth, because I didn't care. I never have and never would. The future she was referencing was not my future but the future she wanted me to have.

"How can you say that? What's going on with you, Riley? Why are you acting like this?"

"Mom, stop with the questions," I blurted.

"I can't believe you," she twisted around the passenger seat to stare at me. "I don't even feel like I know you."

"Just stop, Mom," was all I could really say. I wanted to throw it back in her face, and say "you don't know me" but I resisted.

"I know why you're acting like this, it's because of that stupid boy you're always hanging out with. I told you he was no good, I told you he was trouble," my mother spat, dragging Dean into this. Surely enough, she had her reasons to believe that, but she had it all wrong.

"Maria, just leave her alone. You're not helping," my father finally spoke up, knowing she had crossed the line.

That made her stop. She turned back around, and pouted in her seat, like a toddler. I couldn't believe we actually shared the same DNA.

As soon as we got home, I bolted upstairs and locked myself in my room. The echo of my parents bickering drifted through my walls. Eventually, the fighting stopped, and was followed by the sound of a car zooming off. Probably my mother, giving up again, and going back to her natural habitat; work.

My father was pacing around his office. I could feel the vibrations flow through the floor. He probably wanted to speak with me, but knew that I needed my space. He always put up with a lot, which was why he looked older than he really was. That partially was my fault. Unintentionally, I always found some way to put him through hell.

The hours drifted by, and I continuously held onto the video tape. It was heavy with importance, and I guarded it with my life.

It was worth it, whether my father was willing to accept that or not. He would thank me later on.

The door bell rang at exactly 2:53. That was the first time I left my room all afternoon. I crept into the corner, hidden by the stair railing, and observed as my father answered the door.

"Hello Mr. Jennings. Is Riley around?"

"Dean, hi," my father nervously replied. "Now's not a good time."

"Oh," Dean mumbled. "I guess I'll come back later."

My father slowly shook his head. "Riley may be grounded for a while. You'll just have to wait to see her in school."

"I heard what happened sir . . . I can't wait three days," Dean said, desperately and eagerly.

"I'm sorry, but rules are rules."

Dean sighed. "I understand, sir. Just tell Riley I dropped by will you?"

"Of course," my father modestly replied before closing the door.

That was my signal to bolt back into my room. I locked my door, and creaked open my bedroom window. After everything that had happened today, the cloud of awkwardness that surrounded us was now too high in the sky to care about. When Dean was in clear sight, I called out for him.

"Riley? What are you doing?"

"I want to go with you," I croaked, swinging one leg out the window frame.

Dean scratched his head, obviously baffled by my spontaneous idea. "To where?"

"Anywhere. As long as we go," I replied, climbing onto the ledge.

"Riley, you're already in enough trouble," Dean warned. "You can't afford to get in more trouble."

"I don't care," I replied. "You wanted to see me, right?"

"Well, yeah . . . but not like this. I wanted to sit down and talk, not help you sneak out."

"We all have to make compromises."

He didn't say anything after that, so I assumed that he gave up trying to stop me. Right now, I was being stubborn and rebellious; two traits I had never embraced before.

Climbing down the ledge, I made grabbed onto the awning and lowered myself to the ground. Dean grabbed my waist and helped me down so I wouldn't break my neck or anything. I walked towards his motorcycle and strapped on the passenger helmet.

"Well, what are you waiting for?" I questioned, as I straddled the seat.

Dean sighed before reeving up the engine. He wasn't pleased with me . . . nobody was. But that didn't matter. None of it did.

"Where do you want to go?" Dean screamed above the loud mechanical rumble.

"You choose."

Dean, who somehow knew of all the best secret places, took us to an abandoned alley. We sat against on the cold ground, pressed our backs against the wall, and listened to the echos that traveled through the hallowed path.

"Why did you do it?" Dean finally asked, his voice ringing clearly.

"I had to," I muttered. "It was the only way." I didn't need to explain anything to him, somehow he already knew everything.

"But it wasn't. You could have done it differently. You really messed up, Riley," Dean scorned, with disappointment. "You ruined your perfect record, you disobeyed your father, but you don't even seem to care."

"I do care." I narrowed my eyes down at him.

"Then act like you do!" He looked at me, his eyes distraught and pained.

I huffed, unsure of what to say. Finally, I just let the words roll of my tongue. "It was worth it, okay? I'm willing to pay the price. I didn't come here to get judged or scolded by you, I wanted to get away."

"Sorry," Dean glumly replied. "I just wish I heard it from you, not from some random kid in the hallway. I was kind of surprised and hurt that you didn't tell me you were going to do it."

I gave him a meek, half-smile. It was a bittersweet feeling, knowing he obviously cared about me but didn't want to be with me. But I fought against the lousy feeling that hung in the pit of my stomach. Even though I couldn't be with him, I was still happy to have him in my life.

"Sorry, I was going to tell you, I just never got around to it . . ."
He briefly paused. "Did it hurt?"
"It always does. But again . . . it was worth it."
Dean gave me his warm crooked smile. "I'm glad you're okay."
"I'm glad I did," I sighed.
We sat in silence for a few more minutes. There wasn't much left to say at that point. Right now, everything just needed to soak in. Dean eventually took me home.
"You can just drop me off at the corner," I said, as he slowed the motorbike down.
"Well I guess I won't see you for a few days," he mumbled after he cut the engine.
"I guess so."
"Take care of yourself, okay Riley?"
"I'll do my best," I replied, handing him my helmet. "I'll see you around."
I walked away, and climbed back up the wall of the house, and into my room. I listened as the distant roar drifted farther away, before turning away, and entering my time of solitude.

CHAPTER 17

"Dad?" I knocked on the locked door of my father's study.

It was Wednesday morning, the first official day of my suspension.

I had a sleepless night full of tossing and turning. Of course, I was embracing this new attitude of mine but a dreadful feeling rested in my core. While I couldn't identify the source of it, it filled me up with unbearable, emotional misery.

I heard a click through the door knob, followed by the appearance of my weary father.

"Riley," he muttered with a husky voice. "Come in."

My father stalked around his large, oak desk, and plopped down into his leather chair. He rolled up the sleeves of his cotton shirt, crossed his arms, and leaned back. My father pointed for me to take the seat facing his desk, but I was too nervous to sit. So I hovered over him, shifting my weight from one leg to another.

Dad looked up at me, waiting expectantly for me to speak. But I couldn't get the words out, because I didn't know where to begin. Anytime I came close to explaining myself, I would look into his tired, crestfallen eyes, and choke up.

He wasn't angry, nor bitter. But knowing he was disappointed and hurt was more painful than words can describe. The success of the video take gave me glory, but the sorrow of my father filled me with guilt.

Although I was disgusted with myself, I still didn't regret what I did . . . I just hated the fact that I hurt a person I loved.

With a shaky hand, I pulled the video tape out of my sweatshirt pocket and placed it on his desk.

"I'm really sorry, Dad, for everything," I whispered. "I hope you understand."

My father's eyes widened with shock and relief that my suspension hadn't entirely gone to waste, but I escaped to my room before he could respond.

The hours drifted by, but my father never came to talk to me. At this point, I had no idea what his reaction was to the footage captured on tape. So as I waited, I hoped and prayed for the best.

It was mid-afternoon when somebody knocked on my door. Initially, I thought it was my father coming back to discuss the matter at hand. To my surprise, it was Dean.

"Hey Riley," he leaned against the doorway, "your dad let me in so I could drop off your chemistry homework for the week." Dean handed me a green folder full of various pages and assignments.

"Thanks," I meekly replied. There was a brief, awkward pause of silence, so I finally said, "Would you like to come in?"

"Sure," he mumbled, taking a step forward. "I've never seen your room before."

The only boy who had ever been in my room before was Blake. For some reason, I always felt vulnerable when a guy was in the room where I slept and dressed. It was almost as if all my hidden secrets were being revealed in one square space. By natural instinct, I kept the door open just a crack, as my mother used to make me do whenever Blake came in.

"So you're a neat freak," Dean concluded, running his hand over my spotless vanity table.

"Yeah, I guess so," I shrugged.

Dean wandered over to my bed, and tugged on my indigo blanket. "I swear I could bounce a quarter off of this."

I crawled onto my bed, wrinkling the perfect bedding Dean had just commented on. I crossed my legs, and hugged my pillow tightly.

"I gave my dad the tape," I informed.

"Really?" Dean raised his dark eyebrows as he sat down on the edge of my bed. "What did he say?"

I shook my head. "I don't know. I left before he got the chance to say anything."

"So what happens next?"

I shook my head again, and gave my pillow a big squeeze. "I guess we'll just have to wait and see."

"I guess so," Dean glumly replied as he got up and strolled over to my book case. "God, you read a lot." Dean pulled out my paper back copy of Catcher In The Rye, and started skimming through the worn pages.

"You can borrow that if you want."

"Already read it," he answered, as he slipped it back into the shelf. He took his leather jacket off, and leaned against the book case. "You know, school was kind of lonely today without you there."

"Really?" I tried my best to suppress the little bit of excitement I had.

"Yeah, I mean you're my only friend there," Dean replied. "And I missed you."

That time I couldn't hide my excitement, so I allowed my smile to shine on. Obviously, he had just pointed out that we were no more than friends at this point, but that didn't change the fact that he missed and thought about me.

"I missed you too."

Just then, there was a knock on the ajar door. "Can I come in?" My father asked, peering into my room.

"Yeah sure, Dad."

My father gracefully sauntered into my bedroom, nodded to Dean, then took a seat in the chair by my desk.

"Good, now that you're both here, we can discuss this."

"Discuss what?" Dean politely asked.

My father pulled the video tape out. "This. I just finished watching it. As disappointed as I am that you disobeyed me, I'm glad you did it Riley. I never want you to ever do that again, but in this case, you did what we needed to be done. Now that we have the evidence, I say we take action. I think it's time I draft and file a lawsuit against Blake."

My tears welled up ever so slightly. I had anticipated those very words for such a long time, and now, it was finally happening.

"This is very big and very serious. From now on, we have to be extreme careful with everything that happens. Lawsuits can take up to several months before they are brought to court, so we have to be on our top game in that amount of time. Because it may take months for us to get a court trial, I need you to still watch out for Riley, if you can Dean."

"I would be honored to, sir," Dean righteously replied, standing up taller.

My father smiled warmly, causing wrinkles to appear at the corners of his mouth. He took his glasses off and rubbed his tired eyes. "Blake obviously has an abusive personality type, so who knows how he will react. Especially with the amount of time given from his notification of the lawsuit to the first court date, he could do anything. I'm obviously very apprehensive about this situation, because I don't want Blake to go psychotic with anger. I can't allow Riley to become the next one murdered by her abusive ex . I'm asking for a lot, Dean, but I'm desperate."

The word murder sent chills down my spine. I could picture it now; Blake sneaking in through my bedroom window, his crazed eyes filled with fury and bestiality, his hand holding a gun or knife, and his terrorizing movements as he assassinated me until the light left my life and everything around me was dark.

As terrifying as the future was, it also held prospect . . . a prospect too good to let fear take away from me.

Dean ran a hand through his dark locks. "It's not too much to ask for, sir. I feel the exact same way."

"Thank you so much Dean," my father said, as he went over to shake Dean's hand. "I'm eternally grateful. Please, let me pay you for doing this. I owe you for everything you're doing to help me and my daughter."

"Please, Mr. Jennings, I don't want your money. I want to do this more than anything, I don't need to be paid," Dean said, releasing my father's grip. "I want Riley safe just as much as you do."

My heart raced slightly at the sound of his words. But I took a deep breath, and told myself to pull back. Right now, with everything that was about to happen, I couldn't focus on my impractical longing for my knight in shining armor.

"Are you sure?"

"I'm positive," Dean confirmed. "Keeping Riley safe and alive is payment enough."

"Okay then. Thanks again, Dean. Really, I can't thank you enough," my father appreciatively said once more.

"You're welcome sir. It's my pleasure," Dean warmly replied, with sparkling dark eyes and a handsome smirk.

"Well, I should probably get to work on drafting the lawsuit. The sooner we file it, the sooner we can put Blake behind bars," my father said eagerly. "I'll leave you two be."

My father left with an extra bounce to his step. All of this reassurance and hope for a promising future had put him in a satisfying disposition. It was refreshing to see my father lighten up for once, instead of his usual dark brooding.

"Dean, thank you so much for everything. I don't know what I would do without you," I admitted.

"I'm always here for you, Riley. No matter what," Dean replied, sitting next to me on my bed.

I pulled my knees up to my chest, and rocked back and forth. The combination of terror and thrill for the future filled me with unusual anticipation.

"Well I should probably get going. I'll stop by tomorrow, and check up on you. Maybe we could go out for a bit. You could probably use the fresh air," Dean said. pulling on his leather jacket.

I got up and followed him out of my bedroom door. "Thanks again, Dean. It really means a lot. I'll see you tomorrow."

"Goodbye Riley," Dean replied, as he zipped up his leather jacket and flew down the stairs.

When Dean was out the front door, I decided to go and join my father in his study. My father, sitting behind his large desk, was fervently scribbling on his law paper with a fountain pen. As he worked, he tugged at his salt and pepper hair, and bit down on his bottom lip.

"How's it going, Dad?"

He looked up, with wide eyes. "Really well. I should be done by tomorrow night."

"Can I ask you something?"

"Sure, go ahead."

I sighed. "What was it like? Watching the video tape?"

My father gradually put down his pen, and loosened his tie. "Horrifying actually. I always tried to picture what it would look like . . . but actually seeing it with my own eyes was worse than I could ever imagine." My father chocked up, trembling on each syllable. "But I'm glad I saw it. I couldn't avoid it any longer. I have to accept the truth if I want the court to do the same. My biggest hope is that you'll never have to experience anything like that ever again. "

Without thinking, I went around and threw my arms over my father. "I love you Dad. Thank you so much."

"I love you too, Riley," he replied, stroking my hair with his fingers, before pulling away. "You know, now that we're bringing this to court, we're going to have to tell your mother."

"I know . . ." I grunted. We couldn't hide it from her any longer. As my parent, she deserved to know. Even if at times it seemed like she didn't have my best interest at heart. "What about Charlie?"

"Eventually, he will have to know as well. But when the time is right. However, she comes first."

"Dad, can you please tell her?" I whined. "You know we don't see eye to eye."

"If you can't tell your own mother, how do you expect to tell a whole jury? Think of it as a little test," my father reasoned. "We will tell her together, okay?"

"Okay," I mumbled.

"We can tell her tomorrow. She called not too long ago, saying she had to work late. Come on, help me start dinner," he sat up, and patted my back as we exited his study, "I'm thinking pasta."

"That's the only thing you know how to make," I pointed out.

"Then pasta it is," my father concluded, with a big grin.

CHAPTER 18

T hursday night, at dinner, we dropped the bomb.

Since my father had taken two days off in a row, he had to go in for work. I was stranded home alone for the day, tormented by the news I would soon deliver. I prepared for the worst, and hoped for the best.

Charlie was at a friend's house when we had dinner, so Dad and I seized the chance.

"Maria?" My father's voice was soft and gentle. "There's something we need to discuss."

"What is it?" My mother's smile soon faded, as we all exchanged dark, serious glances. "What's wrong?"

My father cleared his throat and raised his eyebrows at me. Obviously, he wanted me to start. I nervously looked down at my plate, and shifted a lonely pea back and forth with my fork.

"Mom, you know Blake, right?" I foolishly asked, even though I knew the answer. Ever since I was a little girl, I had the tendency to crack under pressure.

"Of course," she muttered, suspiciously.

I felt my lungs tighten, and my temperature rise. I lifted my eyes for a split second, only to see my mother glaring at me with brooding eyes. Now, I also felt nauseous . . . great.

"And you know how he was my boyfriend for a while?" I choked a little, beating around the bush.

"Yes . . ." she growled, as she grew more impatient with my idiotic questions.

With each pause, each breath, I became more terrified. May I remind you, my mother was not the most level-headed, under-standing person. She was prone to break downs, panic attacks, and temper tantrums. God only knows how she would react to this news.

"And you remember how I used to fall a lot, and get lots of bruises and cuts?"

My mother crinkled her eye brows together. "What does that have to do with anything? I thought we were talking about Blake?"

She wasn't getting it, but I couldn't bring myself to spell it out for her. It hurt too much; physically and emotionally. My left temple, where Blake had last struck me days before, throbbed with aching memories.

"Well, what is it?" My mother urged, but I was in an everlasting tongue-tie.

"Maria," my father lowered his gritty voice, as he leaned forward. "She never fell, not once. Every time she came home all battered and bruised . . ." he paused, forcing the words out. "Blake did it."

She blinked her eyes a few times. "Blake?" She didn't sound sur-prised, just more confused. "I don't understand. Are you implying that he hurt Riley?"

My father sighed. "Exactly, yes."

"I don't understand. Blake is such a nice, well rounded young man."

I couldn't allow anyone, especially my mother, to think of Blake in that way. He was nothing but a sick bastard; a monster.

"Obviously, he's not," I snapped, an eruption of anger building inside of me.

"So he lost his temper, dear, and he hit you once or twice. Big deal," she shrugged it off, as she sipped her red wine. "Don't be so dramatic. It happens all of the time."

Now, I had really lost it. I slammed my fist into the table, causing the dining wear to tremble. How could she say that? Play it off like it was nothing. Was she that cruel, that naive, that goddamn ignorant? Who was she? She certainly was not my mother. A mother would protect her offspring, not turn a blind eye.

"Riley," my mother screeched. "Control yourself!"

"Are you that daft?" I asked, ignoring her order.

"Stop it, Riley, you're acting like a child."

My father cowered to the side, as our claws came out. He knew when it was best to intervene.

"No, Mother, you are. It wasn't just once or twice. I came home with cuts and bruises almost every fucking week. Don't you get it? Blake abused me," I snapped, finally saying it out loud.

"You're overreacting. I'm sure it wasn't that bad."

There were so many things I could have said, but all I could do was laugh. Something about this conversation with my disturbed mother was so absurd that it was almost humorous. The more I thought about it, the funnier it became.

"Riley, stop it," my mother ordered, but I couldn't. She turned to my father, with blazing eyes. "What the hell is wrong with her?"

Between my bouts of laughter, I said, "It's just so funny, because you're such a bitch!" I cracked up again. "It's unreal!"

That really pushed my mother over the edge. Her mouth dropped, and her eyes widened. I could tell that she was endlessly screaming at me, by the way her lips feverishly moved. But thanks to my roaring laughter, I couldn't hear a word she was saying.

"Riley, go to your room," she screamed.

"Gladly," I chuckled through my big grin.

I laughed all the way up the stairs. But as soon as I locked myself in my dark room, it wasn't all that funny anymore. I stood there; limp, lonesome, dead inside.

Blake abused me. Blake abused me. Blake abused me.

The phrase I had just spoken echoed in my head.

Everything suddenly felt dark, hallow, and gloomy. Somehow, I ended up on the carpeted floor, holding my churning stomach.

"How could you hide this from me?" I heard my mother screech through the floor.

"Because I knew you wouldn't take it seriously," my father rebutted. "And you just proved that I was right."

"Well, it obviously must be serious if you feel the need to bring this to court!" She exclaimed. "Paul, we're married. You have to tell me these things! Our daughter is in trouble. She doesn't need a judge, she needs a therapist!"

I heard my father loudly grunt. He did that sometimes when he was frustrated and lost for words.

"You know what really pisses me off? You'll listen to your husband, but you refuse to even hear your own daughters cry for help. She needs you. She told you everything, but you didn't believe her until I confirmed it. Maria, you're my wife, but your also her mother. Start acting like it," my father roared in my defense.

"How can I be a mother when I don't even know my own daughter? She's not like this! She's out of control. You saw how she was acting."

"She was acting like a regular teenage girl. She's not an adult, stop trying to make her one," he scorned. "You can't define who she is."

I pressed my hands against my ears, and silently screamed. I wanted them to stop, I wanted the voice in my head to stop, I wanted all of this madness to stop!

Without thinking, I flung my body across the room, and started packing a bag full of clothes, toiletries, and money. I just needed to escape this chaos.

My fingers quickly dialed Lucy's number. The sound of her automatic voice message caused me to throw my phone on the ground in frustration. With shaking hands, I delicately picked my phone up from the floor. Trembling, I walked over to my desk and pulled out the school student directory. Then, I did something I had never done before.

"Hello?" The voice answered after several ringtones.

"Dean? I need you to pick me up," I whimpered into the mouth piece.

"Riley?"

"Please, Dean, I need you to come and get me," I sobbed, unable to control myself any longer.

"What happened?" He asked, but I couldn't answer through my blubbering. "Okay, okay, I'll come get you. Stay where you are."

I heard the phone line click off.

"Please, hurry," I whispered into the phone to nobody.

As soon as I released my phone, I collapsed on my bed and silently hummed to myself, hoping to block out my parents' continuing argument. I wasn't sure how much time had passed when I heard the roaring engine pull up, but my parents were still bickering.

With weak arms and legs, I took my backpack and climbed out of the window. Dean was there below, spotting me as I made my jump from the ledge. Seeing his handsome, concerned face in the shadows of the night and trees caused me to break into hysterics yet again. He pulled me tightly into an embrace, held me so closely that I could feel his heartbeat on mine.

"Shh, it's okay," he cooed, as he stroked my hair that draped down my back. "Everything's going to be okay. I'm here."

I continuously sobbed, letting the tears and snot pour out of me. I didn't care though, and neither did Dean.

"It's going to be alright," he whispered, holding onto me. "Tell me what happened."

I loosened my grip, and opened up a bit so I could face him. I took a deep breath and tried to explain, but I couldn't articulate my words.

"Okay, shh, it's okay," he hushed, as he pulled me back in.

We stood there in the lawn, in the cover of the night, holding each other. Finally, I composed myself, but I never felt rushed to explain what was going on or what was wrong. Dean was a good sport about it all, and he knew how to make a person feel better.

"I see you've got some stuff with you," Dean pointed to my backpack, and I meekly smiled. "Where am I dropping you off?"

"I don't know where I'm headed," I shrugged, as I contemplated my escape. "I guess you could take me to the train station."

"You're leaving? Like actually running away?"

"I guess. I don't really have anywhere to go. I just can't stay here," I muttered.

"Well . . ." Dean grumbled. "You could stay at my house for a while. It's better than having you in some random town miles away."

"I couldn't put you out like that, I don't want to be a burden," I shook the idea off.

"You wouldn't be. My mother loves having guests," he added. "Please. I have to make sure you're safe."

"I couldn't . . ."

"You could. Please, Riley, for me. Just so I can sleep at night, knowing you're okay," he begged, with sincere eyes.

I sighed. He was really set on this idea. "What about your brother?"

"I'll make sure he doesn't bother you," he confirmed. "He just needs to get to know you better. This would be the perfect opportunity."

"I can't just stay with you," I stammered.

Reaching for my backpack, Dean slung it across his shoulders. He took my hand, and led me towards his motorcycle.

"You can and you will . . ." he stopped in his tracks as if he forgot something, then shook his head. "I'll call you dad later and let him know where you are."

"Dean, stop," I spat, pulling my hand out of his, despite wanting to hold onto it for just a moment longer. "This is ridiculous. I can't stay with you. As close as we have become, we're not this close."

He crossed his arms. "Oh please, that's such bullshit. For fuck's sake, I have your boogers dripping on my leather jacket," he said, with a little laugh. "Come on, Riley. Just stay with me, it'll be fine."

The idea did sound nice. My lustful desire for him was pulling me towards this proposal. But I hadn't lost all of my sensibility.

"No, Dean . . . I don't know anything about your family. The only person I've met is your brother," I rolled my eyes. "And he's a complete ass."

Dean ran a stressed hand over his face. "Riley, what's the problem? It's me, Dean. Why are you acting like we've never met? It's not like you're staying with a stranger.

"Sometimes, you feel like one," I admitted, thinking of inevitable distance that was still between us.

Dean laughed. "Riley, this is ridiculous. I know you, you know me. We know everything about each other."

I crinkled my eyebrows and thought of the mystery of the Black Knights.

"Do I though?" I questioned.

Dean let out a heavy sigh. "If you agree to stay with me and not run away or live on the streets, I'll tell you everything," he lowered his voice and took a step closer. "Everything . . ."

CHAPTER 19

"Are you sure your parents won't mind that I'm staying?" I asked, in a sudden panic as we walked up the cobble stone path leading to his quaint, country house.

"Promise. My mom loves this kind of stuff," Dean reassured.

The moment we stepped inside, a warm glow of light and heat hit us. Dean took off his leather jacket, threw it onto the couch, and called out for his mother.

Mrs. Marks stepped into the living room from the kitchen. As soon as I saw her, I knew where Dean got his good looks from. She was a petite, exotic beauty. There were long, voluptuous curls in her dark, stallion mane. Her skin had a deep, olive coloring, and her eyes were as black as night. Her good looks out-shined the nurse scrubs she wore.

As she wiped her hands with a dish towel, she took a good, long look at me. "Who's your friend?" She asked politely.

"Mom, this is Riley. She's from my school," Dean introduced. "She needs a place to stay tonight."

Mrs. Marks extended her long, slender hand to me. "It's nice to meet you, love. I've heard so many wonderful things about you.

We don't have a guest bedroom but one of the couches in the living room is actually a pull-out bed. I hope you don't mind."

"It's alright, I don't mind at all," I replied, with a soft smile. I didn't need a room at the Ritz, I just needed a place to rest my head.

"Wonderful, you're welcome to stay as long as you'd like."

Dean was lucky to have such a kind woman as his mother, unlike the bitch of a mother I had. I got the sense her and Dean were very close, which would explain his soft sensitivity. While their home was small, it felt like it was filled with love.

"Thanks, Mrs. Marks," I modestly replied.

"Please, call me Josephine," she insisted with a warm smile.

Dean plopped down on the couch, and picked up his brother's carving knife. "Where's Alex?"

"Where else?" Josephine rolled her eyes. "Out with the boys, of course."

Dean moaned. "Right . . ."

"Well, I should turn in for the night. I've got a long day at the hospital tomorrow," Josephine said, brushing herself off. "Dean, can you help Riley with the bedding?"

"Sure, Mom."

"Thanks sweetie," she lightly kissed the top of his head. "It was nice to finally meet you, Riley."

"You too," I replied, but it was too late; she was already out the room and down the hallway.

Dean spread out across the couch and made himself comfortable. "See? I told you she was cool."

"Yeah, she is. I like her, she's sweet," I mumbled, as I nervously lowered myself onto the chair across from him. But that was a real understatement; she was everything my mother was not. "What's your dad like? Will I get to meet him?"

"Not tonight," he quickly replied, then paused briefly. I crinkled my eyebrows at his unusual reaction. "Well, I should go get the bedding for the pull-out couch."

He jumped up from his extended position, and exited the room. When he came back, he had arms full of sheets, blankets, pillows. Together, we made up the bed that pulled out of the couch; smoothing down the sheets, fluffing the pillows, and throwing down the covers. As I slipped underneath the blankets, I realized that this was just as, perhaps even more, comfortable than my bed at home.

Dean cleared his throat as I snuggled up under the covers. "Do you want to borrow some of my clothes to sleep in? I can't imagine you're too comfortable in jeans."

I nodded in response, and watched Dean leave the room once more. I was going to mention that I had packed extra clothes, but the idea of sleeping in a guy's clothes was sort of appealing. Early in our relationship, Blake gave me his varsity football jacket. I proudly wore it every day, until football season started. I took it as a symbol of our relationship; that he was mine and I was his. I found myself sniffing the sleeves during class, just to have Blake's scent fill my infatuated nostrils. That was when things between us were good.

Dean came back into the room with an over-sized cotton shirt and boxers.

"Thanks," I murmured. He smiled warmly in response. I kept still, waiting for him to leave so I could change, but he never did. "Mind turning around?"

"Oh, yeah, sorry," he stuttered, as he turned his back.

I quickly stripped down to my underwear, and stopped for a moment. Dean was only a few feet away from me while I was nearly naked. Rushing, I pulled the baggy clothes on, but tripped as I tried to shove my legs through the boxer shorts. Crashing down, I yelped, causing Dean to instinctively turn around.

"Riley, are you okay?" He blurted just as he turned around. He looked down at me in my underwear and baggy shirt, jumped, and spun around. "Oh shit! Sorry!"

I had never blushed so much in my life. Thank God, he couldn't see my face. Regaining myself, I successfully pulled the shorts on. "It's okay. Sorry, I'm decent now."

Dean hesitantly turned around. His face was still flushed like mine. As the crimson left his face, the intensity in his eyes did not. I couldn't help but wonder why he was looking at me differently. Did he like what he saw? Was he repulsed by it? I had to stop myself from asking pointless question. Why did it matter anyway. He was not, nor would he ever be with me. Whether he was attracted to me or not, we would forever be just friends.

We both sheepishly lowered ourselves onto the bed to sit. Obviously, we were still embarrassed about what just happened. Dean drummed his fingers against his thigh, and clicked his tongue a few times. Eventually, he hit the light switch, reached over to the coffee table and grabbed the television remote.

I watched as the tiny figures danced in the reflection of his eyes. He surfed the channels briefly, pausing here and there, before starting up again. He finally stopped on a Japanese game show.

"Is this okay?"

"Yeah, it's fine," I said, tucking a lock of my hair behind my ear. I was wondering when we would have the talk, but I didn't want to push it. I knew it was coming though.

But not too long after, I fell asleep.

A loud slam woke me up in the middle of the night. Startled, I quickly threw the blankets off of me. I searched the pitch black living room, scanning for the cause of the sound. I saw the front door swinging back and forth, as the cold winter breeze drifted in from the screen. As I got up to close it, I assumed that the wind was strong enough to blow it open.

It was not the strong wind that caused the door to slam; it was two muscular men.

I caught a glimpse through the screen door of Dean and his brother, Alex, fighting in the lawn. They grunted as they punched and strangled each other. From where I was standing, it looked like a pretty fair fight. Alex was bigger and stronger, but Dean was swifter and quicker.

I crept into the shadow of the door way, knowing it would be best if I wasn't seen.

"You don't even care anymore," Alex yelled, pulling his brother into a head lock.

"Damn right I don't," Dean growled, as he broke free.

They parted, and heaved over as they caught their breath.

"All you do care about is your stupid music and that girl."

Dean coughed. "Hey watch it, she's just not some girl. She means a lot to me."

In the darken overcast, I smiled a grin nobody would ever see.

"And your brothers don't?"

"They aren't my brothers," Dean spat. "Only you are my brother."

Alex charged him, and sucker punched Dean square in the jaw, causing him to collapse on the ground. "They became your brothers as soon as you pledged in."

"Well, now I want out," Dean rebutted. He got on his hands and knees, and tried to push himself up, but Alex kicked him back down.

"You're a disappointment . . . to me, to the gang, and to Dad," Alex groaned as he took a few steps back. "I hope your happy with yourself."

"Believe me, I am," Dean gritted as he stayed perfectly still.

When I saw Alex storming towards the house, I ran for the couch. I let the blankets cascade on me, and I shut my eyes close. Within moments, I heard Alex's boots clunking on the floor. The clunking slowly approached the couch, followed by the sound of heaving breathing. Soon, I was aware of his presence, hanging over me.

"She ruined everything . . ." he whispered to himself, assuming I was asleep.

Then, I heard Alex's boots again, as their loud sound grew farther away. After I heard him go up the stairs, I opened my eyes.

I sat up for a moment, soaking in it. Alex was definitely holding in some extra hostility. From what, I didn't know. But obviously it was something big . . . something bigger than just me.

"Oh . . .you're up," Dean muttered, as he stumbled into the room. "I'm sorry, did we wake you?"

I shook my head, and turned on the light switch. His face was covered in blood, and he was already starting to bruise. "You're hurt."

His hand went to his face, as he touched sticky red liquid. "I'll be okay."

"Let me help you clean up," I offered, as I rose from the couch.

"No, I'm okay. Go back to sleep."

"I can't sleep now, I'm wide awake," I muttered, as I shook my head.

"I'm really sorry we woke you, Riley," he grunted, pressing his hand into his temple.

"Don't worry about it."

We traveled into the kitchen, where I dabbed his bloody face with a wet washcloth. I thought of the first time he took care of me, and cleaned me off. It felt like ages ago. Now, weeks later, the roles had flipped.

"How much did you hear?" Dean asked, as he peered through his swollen eyes.

"Enough," I lied. Right now, I was truly dumbfounded and confused."Are you going to tell me now what's going on?"

Dean narrowed his eyes down. "I guess I have to now. I know I've been kind of avoiding it."

"Yeah, you could say that . . . " I shrugged.

He let out a heavy sigh. "Well . . . I'm not really sure where to begin."

"Start from the beginning," I murmured, folding my hands in my lap.

"Right, right . . ." he began. "The beginning goes way back, before your time and mine. A couple of misfits started the Black Knights back in the 60's around this part of town. I'm not sure why or how, but they came together as one. I think to kind of defend Riverside from all the rich elitists. They weren't called the Black Knight, but someone on the outside once called them that, and I guess they kind of liked it.

I'm sure it started out as harmless, but eventually, the group would find trouble. Or trouble would find them, one or the other. It started out with a few petty crimes; you know, joy riding, small thefts, a couple of fights here and there. And then, it got worse. As the group got larger, the crimes got bigger. They banded together to protect themselves and the people they loved. They were the Robin Hoods of Riverside. This part of town is a rough area that has seen dark times. The Black Knights gave back to the people of Riverside, in their own, weird way.

Anyway, it got to the point where they couldn't stop. The group kept growing and going into what it is today."

I crinkled my eyebrows; I wasn't exactly sure what he was getting at. "I'm not sure I understand."

"Riley," he whispered. "The Black Knights are a gang."

His words echoed in my head but I couldn't hear him over my thumping heartbeat in my ears.All of the pieces were coming together; the initials on the handkerchief, the school record folder Blake gave to his father.

The words on my tongue burned like acid. "A . . . gang? Like the crypts?"

He shook his head. "Not quite. More just like a band of brothers. We value secrecy, brotherhood, justice."

I couldn't breathe. "But you break the law . . . how can you value justice?"

"Riley, the two don't go hand in hand," he cooed. "You should know that."

My head was spinning. I rested my head in my hands and tried to make sense of this all. "And you . . . you've done this stuff?"

He shrugged ever so slightly. "Some of those rumors going around the school were true."

I swallowed hard, and shook my head. I honestly didn't know what to think, and I couldn't find the words. Why did this freak me out so much? All I knew of gangs were the terrible things they were associated with: greed, violence, crime. But Dean was far from terrible. At times, it felt like he was the best thing that ever happened to me. Had I been wrong about him all this time?

I stared at him with deep eyes, silently, nervously.

"Riley, please say something. Tell me what you're thinking," Dean asked, desperation in his voice.

I tried to say something, anything, but my tongue was tied, my lips were sealed and my lungs were breathless.

He continued. "Riley, I'm not a bad guy. Sure, I've done bad things, but that doesn't make me a bad person. Please, say that you don't look at me any differently," Dean pleaded.

Was he any different? Was he still the same guy I knew? Dean was still Dean. Being in a gang didn't change who he was. But something, in my core, did not feel right. Something told me that secrets were still being hidden, and at this very moment, I didn't want them to be revealed.

Dean was still a mystery to me, a mystery that I didn't want to solve. The truth was terrifying, and too much to swallow at once. What I didn't know, wouldn't hurt me. After all, ignorance is bliss.

"I don't," I whispered, as nausea consumed me. Trying to fight it down, I tried to change the direction of the conversation. "Do you need Advil or anything?"

"I'm okay." Dean looked at me deeply. "Are you okay? You look pale as a ghost."

"I'm fine, I'm fine," I replied, brushing his comment off. I walked over to the sink, ran some cool water and splashed my face. "Do you and Alex always fight like this?" I grabbed a washcloth, rung it under the water, and walked towards Dean to help clean his face a bit more.

"Kind of. We usually fight over other stuff though. This is the second time we've fought about you," he admitted. "The first time was after your birthday."

Suddenly, another puzzle piece fit into place. The day after my birthday, Dean missed school and was covered in bruises. That was also the day that Dean insisted that we stay strictly friends. Blood started rushing to my head, and I couldn't help but wonder if Alex had something to do with that.

"I don't understand," I stammered, pressing deeply into a wound of his face. "Why doesn't Alex like me?"

Dean flinched from the pressure. "Riley, please don't blame yourself, you didn't do anything wrong."

"Then what is it?" I dug my fingers into the washcloth, as I tried to control the volume of my voice.

"Alex is a complicated individual. The whole situation is complicated," he let out a heavy sigh. "Let's not get into this right now. I don't want to burden you with it. Let me handle it."

"How are you going to handle it? By getting beat up again?" My voice cracked, and I knew I needed to pull back. I was pushing the boundaries and was going to know too much too fast.

"You've already got enough on your plate, Riley. I'll take care of this, okay? Trust me," he whispered, grabbing hold of my hand again.

In that very instance, when his chapped, bloody hand held mine, I lost it and broke into tears. I couldn't explain why, but something came over me, and pushed me over the edge. It must have been a combination of the news, the exhaustion, the heartbreak, and the stress.

"Riley, baby, what is it?" Dean cooed, which only made me sob harder.

I tried to speak, but the words refused to come out. I couldn't describe how I was feeling, nor did I want to. After the past year, expressing myself had become an obstacle. After all I had gone through, my silence had become a defense mechanism. And it failed miserably. It never stopped Blake from hurting me, it never got me where I needed to be in life, it never helped in any way.

Dean proceeded to comfort me once more. He pulled me down onto his lap, wrapped his bruised arms tightly around me, and rocked me back and forth. His soft, sweet nature soothed me down to mere whimpers. As he swayed with my limp body, he began to hum a tender melody that caused my eyes to droop.

"Riley, are you still awake?" I heard him whisper, but I was too tired to respond.

I felt as my body was lifted from the table in the kitchen to the couch in the living room. He delicately placed my head on the smooth pillow, and pulled the covers over me. I allowed myself to start drifting off entirely.

"You'll never know how hard this is for me."

That was the last thing I heard, and the kiss on the top of my forehead was the last thing I felt.

CHAPTER 20

At the crack of dawn, the persistent ring of my cell phone woke me up from my deep, peaceful sleep. My hand followed the noise until it clamped onto the rectangular object. The rest of my body remained perfectly still.

"Hullo?" I grumbled into the mouth piece, eyes still closed.

"Riley? Where the hell are you? Empty bed, no note, nothing!"

"Dad?" I shrieked as I jumped up from my sleeping position. The rapid speed caused me to black out for a moment or two.

"Do you have any idea what you've done? What we were going through? To find our own daughter missing? Your mother practically had a heart attack."

Throwing the blankets off of me, I was greeted by the chilling sensation of the winter weather. I curled my toes together, as I got up to close the living room curtains. The early morning sun hurt my sensitive eyes. Dean must have forgotten to call him; I guess he really did have other things on his mind.

"Did she call the police?"

"Well . . . no," my father admitted.

"Then obviously it didn't affect her that much," I mumbled with hostility, before retreating back to the warmth of the couch.

"That's not the point," my father hissed into the phone. "Tell me where you are. I'm coming to get you."

"No you're not," I demanded, as I dug my fingernails into my bare thigh. "I'm not coming home."

"Riley Madison Jennings, you most certainly are. I'm coming to get you, end of discussion."

"Then you're going to have to come to Canada," I heard my father make a sound out of distress and grief. "Kidding . . ."

"I'm not laughing, this is serious," he sighed. "Do you know what my first thought was when I saw your room empty and your window open? It wasn't that you had run away . . . I would have never expected you to leave like that. I thought it was Blake . . ." His voice trembled a bit at the end, which only made me feel more uncomfortable. I never really knew what to say in these situations; how to apologize, how to feel sympathy, how to comfort the person. No matter how hard I tried, it always came out wrong.

"But it wasn't," I murmured. "Dad, I'm fine, see?"

"That's not enough, Riley. Just please, let me take you home so I can stop worrying about you."

"You don't have to worry, Dad. I'm safe," I paused. He wasn't going to give up; he was too determined. "If I tell you where I am, will you promise to let me stay?"

He coughed. "I'll consider it."

"I'm staying at Dean's," I answered, as I held my breath for his reply.

He sure took his precious time. "Fine. You can stay, but only until Sunday. Make sure Dean brings your homework home today so you don't fall behind in school."

"Thank you," I replied graciously.

He kept the conversation going for a bit, asking pointless questions and drawing his own conclusions. I let him go on, because I knew it made him feel better. As I listened half-heartedly, I picked up the sticky note left on the coffee table: Riley, went to school. My mom is at work, but Alex is asleep. He won't bother you. I'll probably be home before he wakes. Make yourself some food and keep yourself entertained. Dean's sloppy, flawed handwriting was actually kind of refreshing and comforting.

"Well, I'm running late for work. I expect a call later," my father finally resigned.

"Okay."

"I love you," he murmured, almost pathetically.

Tears welled in my eyes, only because I knew I had done it again; hurt the people I loved.

"I love you too, Dad," I replied. "I'll call you later."

And with one click, he was gone and I suddenly felt lonely. The once comforting home now felt like an empty, hollowed house. Without Dean, it wasn't the same.

Time dragged on. One second felt like one minute, one minute felt like one hour, one hour felt like eternity. By the time I showered, dressed and ate, it was only the early afternoon. I became eager and anxious for Dean to come home. I needed a distraction that television and books couldn't provide.

After aimlessly wandering through each room, something grabbed my attention, and pulled me in like a magnetic force. The mysterious photograph was still perched upon the fireplace mantle. The handsome man in the frame peered into my soul with his lonesome, tired eyes. I read the Latin prayer again, before clasping the frame in my two hands. Gently, I peeled the old photograph from the frame.

The edges were rough and worn between my fingertips. The resemblance between Dean, Alex and this man was uncanny. I flipped the photograph to its backside, where a name and date was written: Vincent P. Marks - 9/28/09.

I was intrigued . . . so intrigued that I dropped the frame, and let it shatter into a billion pieces on the floor. I snapped into rush mood, terrified by the damage I had done. I tore through the house, searching for a suitable broom and dustpan.

I found the utility closet near the mudroom. As I rummaged through, I managed to destroy more property of the house I was so kindly welcomed into. I tripped over a misplaced item, and slammed into multiple shelves. An explosion of noise echoed through the house, as object after object crashed and boomed. Broken glass sliced at the bare skin on my foot, but I felt no pain.

"What the hell?"

I turned around, only to see a shirtless Alex glaring at me. His hair was still messy from sleep, and his eyes were lifeless and squinty. Obviously, he was pissed that I had woken him from his beauty sleep.

"I'm . . . sorry, I just . . . and then I . . . fell . . . and tried to . . . and kind of . . ." I miserably explained, as I stumbled through my words and made awkward hand gestures. My mouth and mind refused to align.

"Unbelievable . . ." Alex shook his head. "You can't do anything right, can you?"

He paused, and looked at me expectantly. Did he really want me to answer that? I ended up just kind of shrugging and awkwardly shaking my head. Alex continuously stared at me like I was some freak.

"Why were you in there anyway?"

"I kind of . . . dropped the photograph," I breathlessly answered, only with slight recovery.

Alex suspiciously raised his eyebrows at me, baffled by my unclear response. Awkwardly, I scratched my scalp, then pointed to the living room. When Alex saw the shattered picture frame, he bolted over, and picked up the pieces.

"What the hell is wrong with you?" He scorned, as he delicately lifted the old photograph from the cold, wooden floor.

"I'm sorry . . . I didn't mean to," I weakly apologized. "I was just looking."

"Didn't your mother ever tell you to not touch what isn't yours?"

I stepped out of the dark closet. "I'm sorry."

Alex glared at me, then directed his eyes down to the pool of sticky red liquid below me. "Shit, you're bleeding."

"Oh . . . yeah." I looked down at my blood soaked feet. I hadn't realized how deep the cut was.

Alex sighed, then hurried over. "As much as I'd love to let you bleed to death . . ." he swept me up in his arms with one quick movement. "My mother would kill me if blood got on the carpet."

Alex proceeded to carry me over to the kitchen sink. It really wasn't necessary, I could walk fine without splattering blood all over the place, but I had no complaints to being held so close to his bare, solid body. He hated my guts, but a girl could dream, couldn't she?

Alex managed to stitch me back together in no time. In a blink of an eye, I was cleaned off, sterilized, and bandaged.

"Where did you learn to do that?" I asked in awe, as I took a seat at the kitchen table.

He rolled his eyes, as he scrubbed off his hands in the sink. "My mother's a nurse."

"Right . . ." I slugged over, knowing I had asked a stupid question.

"But I have had a lot of practice," he muttered under his breath.

"Oh yeah? Where?"

That caused Alex to throw down the piece of cloth he was using in rage. I hadn't seen such a temper since Blake. "Why don't you mind your own business and go back to where you belong," he snapped, before storming back upstairs. The clamor of foot steps ended with a slam of the door.

As I sat there in the kitchen, dumbfounded by the quick reaction, I couldn't help but be thankful that I, for once, was not used as a punching bag in a moment of rage. I picked up the cloth he had dropped, only to see that it was twin of Dean's BK handkerchief. Turning a blind eye, I put the handkerchief back in the spot I found it in.

As I meekly exited the kitchen, I checked the clock above the stove - 2:15. Only half an hour until Dean came back from school. But I suffered during those last thirty minutes. The photograph, my ultimate distraction, had been taken from my possession, leaving me with nothing but more pondering questions.

When Dean came barging through the front door, I let out the biggest sigh of relief. I had never been so happy to see someone in my life.

"Dean, thank god you're home!" I squealed as I impulsively threw my arms arms around him.

"Well, hello to you too," he chuckled lightly into my shoulder. "I wish I got a greeting like that every day."

I caught my breath for a moment. "Sorry, it's just been really lonely here without you."

"I'm sorry I had to leave you," Dean replied, his brown eyes glimmering past their black and blue borders. When Dean was injured, he looked even more handsome and disheveled. When I was injured, I just looked like a walking disaster.

Dean began to take off his leather jacket, when he noticed the blood stained on the wooden floor. He then proceeded to scan my body, and stopped at my bandaged foot. He sat me down on the couch, and held up my foot.

"What happened?"

"I fell," I answered. Dean stared at me with distasteful eyes. "This time for real. There was some broken glass involved too, but I'll spare you the gory details."

"Well, you managed to clean yourself up good this time," Dean concluded.

I modestly shrugged. "I had some help. I kind of woke Alex up with the noise. He cleaned me up, then just kind of left. Bare minimum interaction." I left out a few minor details, but I figured there was no need to get Dean involved in something so small and petty.

"Well, I'm glad you're alright," Dean gave my foot a squeeze before lowering it to the ground, "I'm just surprised that Alex was helpful. He's usually pretty useless."

"Yeah, well . . ." I shrugged.

Dean got up from the couch, and carried his belongings upstairs. I was alone again. Dean seemed to be gone for a while, and I was starting to get bored, so I decided to go look for him. From the foot of the stairs I heard yelling.

"She knows too much, she can't stay."

"She's not causing trouble, she's not poking her nose into our business . . . come on, Alex, be reasonable."

I held my breath while listening apprehensively as the brothers bickered on. A dark, sick feeling rested in the pit of my stomach.

"Yes, she has! I know you're crazy about her and all, but you can't deny that she's getting dangerously close."

"You're just mad because she touched Dad's photograph."

And suddenly, it all became clear. Vincent P. Marks was not their brother nor their uncle . . . he was their father.

"I never liked her from the start, Dean. That just pushed me over the edge. How much does she know?"

"Not that much . . ."

"How much does she know?"

"She knows about the gang . . ."

"Does she know about me? Does she know about Dad?"

"She doesn't know much about you, she probably assumes you're in the gang too, but she doesn't know anything about Dad."

"You better keep it that way."

"Alex, I can't keep hiding things from her."

"Don't you get it? This is serious. This is bigger than you or her."

"I know you don't trust her, but I do."

There was silence.

"Don't make the same mistakes Dad made."

Loud foot steps signaled me to retreat. I ignored the stinging pain in my foot as I raced back to the couch. Alex stormed through the living room, blissfully unaware of my presence, and slammed the front door behind him. The second round of footsteps was much slower, much softer, as Dean glumly retired on the bottom step. He sighed heavily, then rubbed his face in distress. His mannerisms reminded me of my father.

"Hey, wanna get out of here?" I offered him my hand, and pulled him up to his feet.

He silently grabbed his jacket and keys, and followed me outside. We suited up for the bike, and climbed on.

"Where to?"

"I think you should take me home," I answered with deep regret. A part of me wanted to stay and be with Dean, but I had caused too much drama within the household. It would be wrong if I stayed.

"You want to leave? But it's only Friday."

"I know, but I miss my family," I partially lied. I did miss my brother and father, but that was not the reason behind my decision. "I should really go."

"I understand, but I'd love it if you stayed," Dean pleaded. "I really like having you around."

The dark helmet that covered my face concealed my big, goofy grin. "If it doesn't work out, I'll come back."

"Deal," he agreed, as he turned on the engine.

I grabbed onto his waist, as the bike accelerated on the hot black pavement. My arms and body felt secure around his.

It was clear to me that things between us were complicated. Love and romance was so close, but felt unattainable, so far from reach. It was not a matter of feeling or emotion, because as it had just been confirmed, we both had it. Something was holding us back. And as Alex had said, it was bigger than him or me.

CHAPTER 21

When we got in, the house was dark, cold, and quiet. The television was playing softly, providing a blue glow for the living room. Approaching the couch, I found my father peacefully asleep. He still had his glasses on, so I lightly lifted them from his face and pulled a knitted blanket over him.

Dean quietly followed me up the stairs. The door to my parents' bedroom was open just a crack, so I peered in, only to find my mother asleep as well. Charlie's door was closed, so I let him be. He would be the last person in this house to disturb us anyway.

My bedroom was just as I left it. The clothes I had thrown in a hurry were still scattered across the floor, used tissues were still moist from the tears I had shed just one night before, and the blankets on my bed had been twisted and tangled.

"Is this the messiest your bedroom has ever been?" Dean asked, flopping onto my wrinkled bed sheets.

"Yeah, I guess."

"Wow, this is nothing compared to my room," he chuckled. It suddenly occurred to me that I hadn't even seen his room, nor any part of upstairs of his house.

Having Dean in my bedroom was not nearly as uncomfortable as last time, but I still felt slightly awkward and anxious. No matter how hard I tried, I couldn't stop my leg from bouncing in anxiety. I even went back to an old habit of mine, and started nibbling on my thumbnail. I sat at the foot of my bed, stiff as a rail.

"So you must be excited to go back to school on Monday," Dean inferred, as he flipped through the pages of one of the books on my nightstand.

"Yeah, I guess," I shrugged. "It's gonna be weird seeing everyone. They all know, don't they?"

Dean dolefully nodded. "A good number of people do. They all seemed to be pretty shocked."

"I guess nobody pegged me as the type of girl who would break the rules and get suspended," I rolled my eyes, disturbed by the constant, concrete stereotypes within my school.

"I don't blame them," Dean mumbled. "But I always knew you were secretly a rebel at heart."

I grinned at the thought of being reckless. "Yeah?"

"Yeah," he grinned back.

In a way, Dean suffered in the same way that I did. People at school labeled him as the bad boy; the misguided, simple-minded kid who was up to no good. Nobody really knew or suspected that he was a sweetheart who loved to read.

Dean uncomfortably shifted around in my bed. He crinkled his eyebrows, stood up, and reached under my mattress. He pulled out my red leather journal. "Hey, what's this?"

"Hey, give me that!" I leaped in the air, and tried to snatch it from him. He teased me, holding it high in the air, far from my reach. "Dean, come on, give it back!"

"What? I can't hear you?" Dean played. "Let's read Riley's inner thoughts."

He untied the ribbon, and thumbed through the worn pages. In a moment of panic, I tackled him to my bed, and grabbed my journal from his hand. I couldn't let him read the entries I had written about him.

After it was back in my possession, I had realized what I had done; I was on top, straddling him. But I didn't want to get off, his black, midnight eyes had put me in a trance. And then, everything from there happened so quickly and so unexpectedly. He reached up, stroked my cheek, and tucked a lock of my hair behind my ear. Dean gripped my waist, and rolled me over so he was on top of me. He bent his neck down, and let his warm breath tickle my skin. Softly and slowly, he kissed me. I felt myself melt under his touch.

"Wait," I huffed, as I broke away. "What are you doing?"

"Doing what I should have done a long time ago," Dean whispered, before kissing from my ear down to my neck.

"But what about everything you said last time . . ." I pushed him off, even though I really didn't want to. "I can't have you coming back tomorrow and taking it all back again."

"Riley, it's not like that," Dean sat up. "Yeah, it's complicated between us. There's a lot fighting against us, but I like you Riley, and I want to make this work."

I sighed, and pulled my knees to my chest. It was finally here, everything I ever wanted with him. And yet, I was afraid . . . no, I was terrified. I should have been flying on Cloud 9, but I was face down in the dirt. Maybe it was because he did hurt me before, maybe it that he was still such a mystery, or maybe I wasn't ready to jump into another relationship after everything I had gone through with Blake.

"Dean, I'm scared, " I muttered.

He turned to face me, and held my hands. "Please, don't be. Please, tell me what to say to make it better. I'll do whatever it takes."

"I just don't know . . ." I replied lowly, letting a tear slip out of the corner of my eye. Why couldn't I just be happy for once?

Dean used his thumb to wipe away the glimmering tear. "Hey, hey, it's okay. No rush, we can take it slow if that's what you need. I just want you to give us a chance, cause I really want you Riley, and I really think we can make this work."

"Okay," I agreed, as I nodded slowly and gnawed at my bottom lip. "One step at a time."

He softly kissed me again, sending a rush of sensation through my body. When Dean kissed me, I could feel his love and passion; that was never the case with Blake. We laid back on my bed, where Dean held me close in his arms as we stared at the glow-in-the-dark stars on my ceiling. We made small talk for a bit, but I let the conversation die out.

"Is something wrong?"

I hesitated, as I silently debated if I should ask the one question that had been bothering me. "No, not really," I lied, deciding against it. Not here, not now. When he was ready to tell me everything about him and his family, I'd be ready with open ears. I wasn't going to pressure him because it wasn't my business.

Dean left not much longer after that because it was getting late. He left me with a soft, tender, melting kiss that would hold me over until Monday at school.

The first day back was stranger than I thought it would be. I had only been gone for three days, but it felt like three years. My morning routine was rusty, and caused me to keep Dean waiting longer than I should have. He sat patiently at the kitchen table, as he watched me scramble around in a rush.

"Let's go!" I sprinted through the kitchen as my bagel popped from the toaster. Keeping my speed, I turned the corner and pushed for the finish line - the front door.

"Don't you need a jacket?" Dean asked from behind me.

In mid step, I froze. "I'm fine, it's not cold."

"No, it's the middle of December," he stated like my father would. "Go get a jacket. You're not getting sick on my watch."

I huffed, and stomped over to the coat closet. Did he want to be late to chemistry? Tearing through the coat hangers, I stopped on the leather jacket that had rested there for a week. Suddenly, I wasn't racing against the clock. The heavy black sleeves fit comfortably around my arms, and the studded lapels framed the tips of my hair.

"How does it look?"

Dean smirked, as the fire burned in his eyes. "Joan Jett would be proud."

I slugged my backpack on, and tried to pick up the pace as I reached for the doorknob. "Can we go now?"

"I think you forgot one thing . . ."

I clenched my teeth in frustration. "What now?"

As I turned back around, Dean pushed me against the door, and pressed his soft lips into mine. My knees were weak, and my mind was giddy.

"Now we can go," he said with a cheeky grin, as he opened the front door for me.

On the outside, I casually kept my cool, but my insides were doing back flips. That boy drove me crazy, and that scared me. An alarming sensation in the pit of my stomach told me to protect myself, and be cautious. I wanted to give him my all, I wanted to let down my guard, but I couldn't bring myself to. The relationship had just begun, and who knows what was yet to come. The last thing I wanted was to get hurt . . . again.

Surprisingly, Dean got us to school on time. The walk of shame through the crowded lobby was unbearable. They whispered and they stared; they gossiped and they glared:

"I heard she beat the shit out of Jimmy Yeens."

"I heard she's failing all of her classes now."

"She used to be so nice. What happened to her? Look at her now."

"She can kiss being Valedictorian goodbye."

"That new kid has changed her. I don't even know who she is anymore."

Dean heard them too, but he had self control as he clenched his fists into balls of anger. He put his arm around me, and held me tightly as we walked.

"Don't listen to them," he whispered in my ear, as I tried to choke back the tears.

We finally reached our chemistry classroom, where I desperately hoped to find a moment of peace. But I never did. At Oxford High, you can never escape from the rumors, not even for a second. I was foolish to think otherwise.

When the bell rang, the only thing I could think about was running as fast as I could away from everyone. But neither Dean nor Lucy would allow that to happen. Lucy pulled me aside, while Dean lingered a few steps behind us.

"I haven't seen you in ages!" She hugged me to the point where I couldn't breathe.

Looking over her shoulder, I gave Dean a nod to go on without me. When he was out of sight, I filled her in on my new love life. Before I could even catch my breath, she choked me again with her embrace.

"Finally! It's about time!"

I shot her a puzzled look. "That's it?"

"You need to celebrate."

"I don't feel like celebrating, Lucy," I admitted, as I pushed my way through the stampede of students in the hallway. "I should, but I don't. Something feels wrong."

"Of course it's going to feel wrong. You just got out of another relationship, and that scar is going to take a while to heal," Lucy reasoned. "Dean's a great guy, we both know that."

"Maybe he's not," I blurted out.

She turned to look at me, her eyes widen in confusion. "What do you mean?"

"There are things I don't know about him, things he hasn't told me," I mumbled in a low tone. "Maybe I don't know him as well as I thought. What if he's not the guy I think he is?"

"What exactly are you referring to? It could just all be in your head," Lucy suggested.

"His family . . . his brother, his father," I stuttered, as I struggled to form sentences. My mouth was paralyzed by my thoughts. "I don't know, it's a long story."

She slowed down, as people zoomed by us. "I don't know what you're getting at exactly but whatever it is, have you asked him about it yet?"

I shook my head. "I almost did, but I don't think it's my place to ask."

"Well, there's your problem. You're no longer his friend, you're his girlfriend," Lucy stated loudly. "You deserve to know these things."

"Can't he just tell me when he's ready?"

"He could . . . but who knows when he'll be ready," she raised her voice. "Riley, I really think that knowing everything will put your mind at ease. Then you actually have a shot at a good relationship." The warning bell rang. "Look, I've got to get to class. If I get one more tardy, Mrs. Peterson is going to whoop my ass. Just think about what I said, and do what feels right."

She left me stranded in the hallway, with a head full of doubt and a heart full of uncertainty. The thoughts in my head competed with the murmurs of others. In that moment, everything became too overwhelming to handle, so I snapped.

"Quit staring, would you?" I screeched at two sophomores who were obviously exchanging rumors. "Mind your own fucking business."

I stormed off, fed up with the people in my school. I knew I had given them even more to talk about, but I could care less at this point. All I wanted to do was rush to the closest bathroom and cry my eyes out until everything around me became insufferably blurry or crystal clear.

CHAPTER 22

I slammed the stall door behind me, and threw my face over the toilet bowl. I heaved a few times, trying to relieve myself of the nauseous feeling that rested in the pit of my stomach.

I came back to school, only to discover my life in ruins.

It was a domino effect; breaking up with my boyfriend triggered my new attitude, which launched a disturbance in the natural order of things, causing this disaster. As I slung myself over the toilet seat and whimpered quietly to myself, I couldn't help but wonder if I had done the right thing.

Sure, being with Blake wasn't healthy. That was obvious. But when I was with him, my life was solid and secure. There was no guessing, no surprises, no turn of events. As much as I hated it, I took for granted the peace that came with it. I was in pain, but I could have suffered quietly.

These days, nothing was quite normal. My family was falling to the wayside of disagreement, my once planned academic path was now a blur, and the fear for my life was growing by the day.

Thinking about this more, another question popped up: who was I? No doubt I was breaking out of the shell I had lived in for so long, but was I the person I pretended to be now? Was I as fearless as I looked and acted? Did I really give a damn?

Of course I did. College still meant everything to me, and certainly I was still scared.

So who was I?

Maybe I didn't fit into either shells. Maybe I was somebody else. Maybe I was nobody.

I pulled myself up from the bathroom floor and went to the sink, where I splashed my face over and over again with cold, bone-chilling tap water. I looked at myself in the mirror, as I always did. My hair was still brown, my eyes were still light, and my skin was still fair.

I endlessly searched myself for some outer change that would match the change I felt inside of me. Despite the alteration of my make up and clothes, my physical appearance still looked the same . . . to me at least. It was hopeless, because I knew no matter what, I wasn't going to be satisfied. So I left.

Stumbling out of the bathroom, I ran into a familiar face. His intimidating, piercing blue eyes and tousled blonde hair passed me by as if I was invisible. He was too absorbed in his newest victim who held on his arm - a brunette, wearing a cardigan and skirt - who went by the name of Emily Carter. Like me, she was in the top 10% of the class. I had been replaced. Scoffing, I shook my head and concluded that some people never changed. I only hoped that Emily wouldn't end up suffering a fate similar to mine.

A few minutes later, I ran into another familiar, but more comforting face. Dean threw his arms around me. I held him close, and nuzzled my cheek into his broad chest.

"Are you okay?"

I sniffled, thankful for his sensitive nature. He always knew when something was wrong, and knew when it was best not to ask about it.

"I'll be fine."

He tucked a lock of hair behind my ear. "I had a feeling your first day back was going to be rough. I got a pass from class, so I'm all yours for the rest of your free period."

"Thanks Dean," I huffed out. "Wanna go sit outside in the courtyard?"

"Won't you be cold?"

Dean gazed at me with his gorgeous, mysterious eyes, which instantly put me in a good mood. Just being around him made me feel better.

I shook my head. "I've got my leather jacket," I winked. "I'm set."

We traveled through the hallways, hand in hand, until we found one of the doors that led out to the main courtyard. It was deserted and quiet, with only nature as our accompaniment. The grass was coated in a thin frost layer, and the bare trees swayed in the breeze. We parked ourselves in the field, and laid down on our backs, side by side.

Dean turned and lifted his head, kissed my cheek lightly, then leaned and rested on his arms for a bit. I couldn't help but look up at him with glazed, starry eyes. His face was so mesmerizing; his dark eyes, his thick eyebrows, his chiseled jawline, his crimson lips, his scars, and his freckles. I wanted to study and memorize every detail of his beautiful face. It seemed like Dean was doing the same for me, except his eyes never broke the connection with mine.

I laid there peacefully, and enjoyed the perfect moment we were sharing. Not everything between us was perfect, but right now, it felt like it was. Unfortunately, our perfect moment had to end. The bell rang, and we were forced to leave the safety of our sanctuary.

The rest of the day I traveled like a ghost, drifting through the shadows as an unseen bystander. I kept my head bent low, so that my hair would hang and cover my face. I wanted to be invisible, as I had been to Blake just hours before. People still talked about the changed, unruly Riley Jennings, but nobody saw her.

Relief struck when the final bell rang at the end of the day. I joined the stampede, eager to escape this never-ending hell. Dean managed to find me in the crowded lobby, then he swept me away towards the parking lot. He slung his muscular arm around my waist and held me close. As we walked towards his parking spot, another couple blocked our way.

"Look who it is, couple of the year," Blake sneered to his new punching bag. She let out a light cackle, and then snapped her gum. Blake stood tall in his football team jacket, proud and threatening.

"Blake," Dean muttered. "Move."

Blake widened his eyes and clenched his jaw. "Make me." Dean curled his hand into a fist in rage, but later released it. He knew better. "Yeah, that's what I thought. Have you two met my new girlfriend? This is Emily."

This is where I'm brutally reminded that no matter who you are in this school, everybody knows everybody.

"As if we all haven't been going to school together since Kindergarden . . ." I muttered under my breath.

He rolled his eyes, as he pulled her thin body closer to his. "She's next in line for Valedictorian . . . now that you're out of the running," Blake snapped at me.

"Who said I'm out? I'm still in it," I raised my voice.

The couple chuckled as if I had said something funny. "You're kidding, right?"

Dean looked at me, asking me to back off with his eyes. But I couldn't help but ignore him. I may have not be the same person anymore, but my values hadn't changed.

"My GPA is still standing, my curriculum and scores are still as they are, so no, I'm not kidding."

"Right . . ." Blake remarked in the midst of chuckles. He gave Emily a tight squeeze, and a slight push. "Babe, why don't you go wait in the truck? I'll be there in a minute."

Emily kissed his left cheek, leaving a faint red lipstick mark. As she pushed through us, she glared at me with intense, competitive eyes.

"Isn't she great?" Blake rhetorically asked, with sparkling eyes.

"Yeah . . . a real individual," Dean mumbled. Obviously, he picked up on the similarities too.

Blake sighed, like a love sick puppy. But he didn't have either of us fooled.

"Yeah well," he paused briefly. "Don't think I've forgotten about you. It's not over, yet."

With a cackle, he walked away with his hands shoved in his pockets. It was unbelievable how sick and twisted a person could be.

Dean channeled his attention towards his bike. Quickly, his face washed over with panic. He hurried to the side of his motorcycle, and knelt down. His fingers dipped into a pool of a dark, oily substance.

"That bastard . . ." he muttered to himself. His voice grew louder. "That bastard!"

Blake stopped in his tracks, and turned around. He laughed wickedly, and twirled a screw driver with his fingers. Everything after that happened all too quickly. Somewhere in between, Dean lost it. He charged towards Blake, fists at the ready, and socked him. Of course, Blake and his hot temper fought back. A crowd of people swarmed to the sides to watch the fair, ongoing fight. Emily got out of the truck, and screamed. About five minutes in, the security guard came and broke up the quarrel. He pulled them apart, and dragged them inside to the principal's office.

"Look what your scumbag of a boyfriend did," Emily cried in fury.

I gritted my teeth at her. "Oh, don't act like Blake is such a saint. You saw what he did to Dean's bike."

"With good reason," she snapped, tugging at her hair.

"Of course . . ." I turned away, shaking my head. I was done with her. She obviously didn't pick up on the vibe, because she kept going.

"You know, Blake told me everything about you too," she spat with fiery confidence. "How you were intolerable and out of line most of the time, and he tried to help you." She smirked, causing me to growl. I gritted my teeth, and tried to fight back the words I longed to say. They sat like acid on my tongue, burning my entire mouth. Disregarding my cold silence, she went on. "I don't blame him, I would have done the same. But it's different between us."

"I'm sure it is," I hissed sarcastically.

She scoffed a bit, insulted by my mockery. "You don't believe me? Blake loves me, he told me he did. I know it's soon, but it's real. He treats me like a queen, because he loves me. Obviously, he didn't feel that way about you."

Her ignorance was bad before, but it had just reached unreasonable heights. I couldn't restrain myself any longer.

"You need shut the fuck up and back the hell off. You think you're so different, well guess what, you're not. So you better watch out, or you're going to end up just like me."

"What, mentally deranged like you?"

Those words stung, like razor blades pressed against sensitive skin. Not because they were harsh, but because they were true.

"Precisely."

I quickly turned on my heel before she could catch my eyes watering. I stormed off to the back of the parking lot, into a corner where I couldn't be seen or bothered by anyone. I pulled out my cellphone and made a call.

"Dad? I know you're probably at the office, but I need you to pick me up," I sniffed.

My father's voice filled with concern. "Riley, what's wrong? Where's Dean?"

"He's in trouble, Dad," I cried into the phone with shaking hands, unable to hold back the sobs any longer. Something had washed over me at once, as if I was being hit by a wave of uncontrollable, painful emotions.

"Riley, what happened? Where is he? What's going on?" He kept asking, over and over again. But I couldn't form words, I couldn't speak. "Okay, okay, I'm coming to get you. I'll be there soon. Stay where you are at the school. I'll come find you," he finally said.

Time seemed to fly as I waited for my father. Crying my eyes out kept me preoccupied. Why I was so upset . . . I couldn't tell you. Plain and simple, I felt lost in this cold, tortuous world.

My father pulled up in his car just before I was really about to lose it. He pulled me into the tight, comforting, paternal hug I needed, no questions asked.

"Dad . . . it was awful," I sobbed uncontrollably as I pulled away from him.

My father sighed. "Are you ready to tell me what happened?"

I tried. Believe me, I really, really tried. But the task nearly seemed impossible. The explanation was lodged in my dry throat. Luckily, the moment came where I didn't have to speak. Dean and Blake, with the universe between them, exited the school with vexed expressions on their faces. Blake gave Dean one last shove as he headed for his car. Dean shook it off, sat down on the stone wall, and held his head in his hands.

My father and I loaded into his car, and we pulled up to the front of the school.

"Son, get in," my father called out to him. "Let's get you cleaned up."

Dean lifted his heavy head, and peered at us through the tinted car window. I gave him a look, egging him to come. He move slowly, with a painful ache, as he lowered himself into the back seat of the car.

"I'm so sorry, sir," Dean mumbled, as the car engine started.

"Dont apologize, you were doing your job," my father replied. "Now, do you want to tell me what happened? The cat has got my daughter's tongue."

From there, the whole conversation seemed to turn into a never-ending rant. I couldn't even bear to listen to it, because it hurt too much. I felt like I was in the middle of a film, having my whole life narrated by a voice from up above, high in the sky.

"Well . . ." my father cleared his throat after Dean finished. "It looks like we've got some work to do."

I looked at Dean through the rear view mirror. His eyes filled with guilt, sorrow, and panic. Something dark was brewing, and it cast a dark shadow over all of us. We all knew what was about to come, and we could only anticipate and prepare for it.

"Yes sir, we do," Dean replied, in a serious, husky voice.

CHAPTER 23

As soon as we got home, Dean and I followed my father into his study.

"What exactly happened, Dean?" My father asked, as he lowered himself into his large leather chair.

Dean paused, looked at me briefly, then sighed. "Blake has a new girlfriend, but he warned us that he hasn't forgotten about Riley."

My father nodded. "I see. Is this what caused the fight?"

"No sir. Blake also damaged by bike," Dean shook his head with disgrace. "I knew I shouldn't have started the fight, but I couldn't help it. Something came over me."

"Did he fight back?"

I scoffed. "Of course he fought back."

My father ignored my comment and turned to Dean. "What happened after?"

Dean clenched his jaw. "Well, we both were dragged into the principal's office. He gave us both warnings and two weeks of detention."

My father shifted uncomfortably in his seat. "Well you know what this means . . ." We both shook our head. "Dean, now that you are involved and the intervention with Blake has been recorded on your school transcript, if you are asked to be put on the stand, you have to go and speak against him," my father explained with a very momentous tone. "Anything in writing that belongs to the state can be used in the court room."

Dean and I both exchanged puzzled looks.

"What's wrong with that?" Dean asked.

My father grumbled, and flipped through one of his law books. "Well, considering your criminal record, it could actually hurt our case and put you into trouble. It all depends on how the judge and jury takes it."

"So it would harm our case more than it would help?" I shrilled.

My father slowly nodded his head. "Unfortunately, yes."

Dean raised his dark eyebrows hopefully. "But I can't do any damage if I'm not called up, right?"

"Correct. But the chances of that happening are slim. I'm sure Blake's father will hire the best lawyer around. These guys mean business, and they know what they're doing and what they're looking for. You can bet that they'll be on their top game."

"Sir, I'll do whatever it takes," Dean replied with a noble manner.

The wrinkles at the corner of my father's lips formed, as he cracked a warm, but hesitant smile. "Thank you, Dean. You must, under all circumstances, stay out of trouble. Especially anything involved with Blake. We can't risk this case taking an alternative turn."

"I completely understand, Mr. Jennings."

"Be prepared, both of you," my father sternly warned. "Everything is about to change. It'll only be a few more weeks until we're in the courtroom. We must all be prepared. Make this time we have count."

I leaned against the dusty bookcase, and crossed my arms. Too much had been happening too soon. It felt like just yesterday I was still with Blake, waking up every morning and fearing the day ahead of me. That was in the past now. A new era had struck - a new life, a new boyfriend, and a new me.

"Mr. Jennings, I hate to change the subject, but there's something I need to ask you," Dean said to my father.

"We're just about done, anyway," my father replied, tugging on the lapels of his jacket. "Sit down you two. What's on your mind?"

Dean awkwardly glanced over at me. He raised his eyebrows a few times, indicating that this was important. "Actually, I wanted to speak to you privately, sir."

I received the message loud and clear, so I excused myself and left my father's study. As I opened the door, I stumbled across a figure who had been lurking in the shadows.

"Charlie? What are you doing?"

He was on his knees, pressed against the frame of the door. His eyes were filled with tears of confusion and fear. "Riley?" His voice cracked, and let out a slight tremble. "What's happening? Why are you going to court? Are you okay? Did you get in trouble? Are you going to be sent away?"

"Oh, Charlie," I pulled him in tightly, and stroked his soft, brunette hair. Obviously, he had no idea to what was going on, but that soon was going to end. "Everything's going to be alright, Charlie. I'm just going through something . . ." I sat down next to him on the cream shagged carpet, took a deep breath, and tied my loose hair up. "Charlie, you remember my old boyfriend Blake, right?"

I watched as Charlie's face light up, then as it quickly fell. "Yeah?"

"Although Blake seems like a pretty great guy, he's not. He's a good friend, son, football player, and son but he wasn't a very good boyfriend," I paused, and swallowed hard. "Blake used to hit me . . . a lot. More than once."

"But . . . you can't hit a girl," Charlie murmured as he tried to process the news.

"Exactly . . ." I took his hands. "That's why Dad is trying to help me. We're going to make sure that Blake can never hit another girl ever again."

Charlie acted like he understood, but I could see in his eyes that he didn't.

"I promise everything is going to be okay. I'm safe, Dad is working really hard, and soon this will all be over with, and we can go back to normal."

Charlie bit down on his thumbnail. "I don't get it. Blake seemed so cool . . . why would he do something like that?"

I let out a heavy sigh. "Despite how people seem, they can prove you wrong. Blake is messed up, and doesn't know right from wrong."

He nodded, as his eyes cleared up. But suddenly, they changed. There was no sadness, no confusion - just darkness and pain. "Does Mom know about this? Or were you not going to tell her, just like you weren't going to tell me?"

He was insulted by our choice to hold off. "No, Charlie, she knows . . . Dad and I were going to tell you when the time was right."

"And when was that going to be, Riley? Next to never?" He stood up in a moment of fury, and towered over me.

"No, when we thought you were ready . . ." I looked up, feeling small and powerless by the angry figure above me. It sent me back into a horrific flashback, where everything felt too familiar.

"I see how it is. I'm sick and tired of being treated like a little kid! Everybody does. Mom, Dad . . . but I never expected you would. Thanks a lot," he spat. He stormed off to his room and slammed his door so forcefully that the whole house shook with the intensity of his pain.

After a few deep breaths, I regained control of my body and pulled myself up from the floor. My father and Dean came rushing out of the office to see what all of the commotion was about.

"It's okay, guys," I muttered. "It's just Charlie. I told him, but he didn't take it too well."

My father removed his glasses and rubbed his tired, wrinkled eyes. "I thought we agreed to wait."

"Well, I found his ear pressed against the door of your study . . . he asked, what was I supposed to do?" I suggested defensively. "He deserves to know. We can't keep him from the truth forever."

"I guess so. He'll come around soon, once it soaks in a bit," my father stated hopefully. "It's a lot for a 10 year-old to swallow." My father paused, pursed his lips, and shrugged. "Actually . . . maybe I should go have a word with him. I'll see if I can try and calm him down." He extended his palm out to Dean. "If I don't see you before you leave, take care."

"Thanks for everything, Mr. Jennings," Dean beamed with respect.

My father paced towards my brothers room, then quickly bolted around to face us. "Before I forget . . . I approve, but let your mother warm up to the idea before you tell her. The last thing we need in this household is more drama," he exclaimed, throwing his hands in the air and waltzing into my brother's room.

I crossed my arms, and gave Dean an intrigued stare. "What was that all about?"

"I asked for his permission to date his beautiful daughter," he replied casually, with that melting, crooked smirk of his.

I bit down on my bottom lip, and tried to prevent my lips from curling into a goofy grin. But my efforts went to waste. He hunched over, held my chin in his hand, and gave my mouth a sweet peck. Each day, he became less of a intimidating mystery and more like a complex riddle. Each day, I felt one step closer to him. Each and every day was as exciting and surprising as the last.

"So, you've got my father's approval . . ."

"And, you've got my mother's approval . . ." Dean continued the banter.

"Now, I've got to earn your father's approval . . ." I said, trying to get him to tell me the story of Vincent P. Marks.

Dean stopped, letting his eyes droop to the floor below him. "That won't be necessary . . ."

A red flag went up in the back of my mind. Even with all the progress we had made, there were set backs and small secrets from the past. "What do you mean? Why not?"

"Just cause . . . don't worry about it, okay?"

"Are you and your father not close?" I asked with a raised eyebrow.

He uncomfortably shrugged. "Something like that."

"Well, I should meet him. He still plays a part in your life, right?"

I was doing it again . . . where I crossed the line and pried when I shouldn't have. But I couldn't help it; Dean made it nearly impossible not to.

"Let it go, you're not going to meet him," Dean snapped for the first time. He had never spoken to me like that. I stood motionless, like a deer in headlights, shocked by his tone. It was the kind of tone Blake would often use before he would physically push me away. He dropped his jaw, and realized what he had done. "Riley, I'm so sorry . . . I didn't mean it like that at all."

"It's okay," I stammered. "You're sensitive about it."

"I am, but still, I shouldn't have reacted like that . . . Riley, I really like you, and I don't want to mess this up. But I don't think I'm ready to open up to you about that."

Why did he have to say that? Now, I wanted to know even more. The mystery of Dean Marks tempted me. But I had to hold back and respect my boyfriend's wishes.

"Okay . . . when you're ready," I murmured.

Dean leaned against the staircase railing, and raised his midnight eyes at me. "Thanks for understanding, Riley. I mean it. Thank you."

I nodded. It was nothing compared to what he had done for me. He had been through and put up with so much. I was happy to do this small favor for him. Dean deserved the very best from me, because that's what he provided for me.

"You're welcome," I modestly replied, giving his calloused hand a slight squeeze.

He gripped my hand tighter. "I just want you to know that I'm all in. You, me, I'm all in."

His words sent a chill down my spine. This amazing, stunning, kind guy who stood before me had told me that he was giving us his everything. How could I not fall into in his arms and melt? I was crazy about him, and as he had just confirmed, he felt the exact same way.

He kissed me, softly but passionately. I wrapped my arms around his neck, and pulled him closer to me. When he kissed me, the world around me seemed to stop. Just me and him; no parents, no siblings, no abusive ex boyfriends.

Suddenly, the sound of a door closing came from behind us, causing us to break apart.

"I don't even want to know . . ." my father remarked, as he put his hand up to shield his eyes from our path.

Dean waited for my father to lock himself in his office before saying, "I think that's my cue to leave."

I desperately wanted to beg him to stay, but this early on in the relationship would have come off as clingy.

"'Wait, how are you getting home? Your bike is still at school."

"I'm going to walk back, " he explained.

I shook my head. "Let my dad drive you . . . you live so far."

"It's a bit of a hike, but I need some time to clear my head," he murmured. "Don't worry, I'm fine."

As usual, I walked him to the door, and let him sweep me off my feet with a tender goodbye kiss.

"Hey, I've been meaning to ask . . . how are you doing in school?" I asked between breaths.

He curiously grinned. "You're asking me now?" He kissed me again, but I pulled away. "Even better since I've started dating you . . . I've got standards to meet if I'm going to be with the future valedictorian."

I kissed him again, overwhelmed by his bright answer.

"Bye," I whispered.

"See you tomorrow," he answered before squeezing in one last goodbye kiss. And with that, he left me on Cloud 9.

CHAPTER 24

The next few days were surprisingly . . . normal. Dean fixed his bike and served his detention sentence quietly. I kept low on the radar and focused on my studies. We both got into the swing of things, and made a regular routine out of our drama-less days.

With all of this carefree time on our hands, Dean and I were able to do stuff together like a normal couple; we had our share of fair snowball fights, snuggled on the couch with a good movie a few times, and even checked out that new Italian restaurant down Parkson Avenue.

For once, everything in my world appeared to be calm and at peace. But of course, it didn't last forever.

One day during lunch, Blake and his posse approached our usual lunch table.

"Lucy, do you mind?" Blake cocked his head at her, urging her to leave. "This doesn't really concern you, now does it."

Lucy clenched her jaw. "What do you want?" she gritted through her teeth.

"Don't worry about it," Blake snapped.

I saw one meathead in the back right corner snicker as he cracked his knuckles. I knew he was just trying to intimidate us -- he wasn't really going to hurt her -- but still, the action was thought provoking enough for me to send her away.

"Are you sure?"

"Yeah, I've got it," I gulped.

She looked hurt . . . even offended that I didn't need her help. It had been more painstakingly clear that since Dean had come into my life, I depended on her less and less.

"Okay . . ." She gathered her belongings, then headed off on her own.

"Finally . . ." Blake flipped his hair, and pointed to her empty seat. "May I?"

"No," Dean snapped firmly, but Blake sat down anyway. His minions crowded behind him, hovering over his broad shoulders.

"What do you want, Blake?" I sneered, slamming my plastic fork down onto the table.

"I'll deal with you later," he snarled, causing a lump to form in the back of my throat. "I first want to have a word with Dean." A wide smirk appeared on his menacing face.

"What? Is this about our fight last week?"

Blake shook his head, and lowered his voice. "You know what this is about . . ."

"Please, do enlighten me," Dean exclaimed, with an overly sarcastic tone.

"Your brother and his little friends fucked up all of our cars!" A chorus of outraged voices joined in. "I don't doubt that you had something to do with this."

"Your issue lies with my brother, not me," Dean spoke calmly. "And that's what happens when people fight fire with fire."

I could see that Dean was trying to fight back a small grin. He may have not been involved or even supported his brother, but he sure was pleased to hear what had come of it.

Blake's face turned a fiery red, as he muttered under his breath and held onto the lunch table with his dear life. It was the only thing holding him back.

"You all are going to suffer for this," Blake spat, as he waved finger at Dean.

"Easy bud . . . look," Dean sighed. "We don't have to make this bigger than it already is."

"Yes we do," Blake sneered, squinting his eyes. "But as you said yourself, this issue rests with your brother, not you. I hardly think it's your place to discuss negotiations."

Dean continuously glared at Blake, and fought his words back. I slipped my left hand under the table, and gave his thigh a comforting squeeze. His tense face lightened up a bit, as he placed his hand on top of mine.

"Well, now that's settled, we can move on," Blake announced. He tilted his head up to his crew. "Do you mind? I'd like a bit of privacy," he said politely. When nobody flinched, his voice grew stern. "I mean it, scram!"

The stooges sprang into action and bolted away.

Blake leaned back in his chair, stole a grape from my tray, and popped it into his mouth. His chewing rhythm was slow and deliberate.

"I got the paperwork in the mail yesterday . . ."

I pursed my lips at him in confusion, even though I knew perfectly well what he was talking about.

"Don't act stupid," he snapped over the clamor of the cafeteria. "Are you seriously going to sue me?"

"If I wasn't serious, I wouldn't be going through all of this trouble to see you locked up behind bars," I replied with equal intensity.

"You're making a huge mistake . . ." Blake scoffed, as he crossed his arms. "Do you even realize what you're getting yourself into? Do you really think your mediocre father stands a chance against one of the best lawyers money can buy? You will lose . . ."

"You haven't won yet," Dean added.

Blake chuckled to himself. "We'll see about that. See you punks in the courtroom in January . . ." He got up, forcefully slammed the chair under the table, and left.

Dean turned to face me, but I couldn't meet his eyes. I could only stare at the one wheat bread crumb that had fallen on the table. Blake's words echoed in my head, and I couldn't help but wonder if he was right . . . maybe we had no shot, maybe all of our time and efforts were going to waste.

Dean didn't speak, he didn't reassure me, didn't tell me not to listen to Blake. He didn't need to. The light kiss he gave me on my cheek was enough to knock some confidence and sense into me.

"Are you going to be okay?" He asked softly. I gave him a small nod. "Do you want to come over today after school?"

"Okay," I mumbled with a slight smile.

And so, when the end of the school day came, Dean and I hopped on his bike and rode off to the other side of town. The ride went relatively fast and smoothly, despite the icy winter roads. His house, just as quaint and homey as I remembered, was coated in a frosty, white layer. Inside, a warm fire was crackling, giving the whole house a smokey, orange glow. I had only been here a few times, but this house felt more like home than my own.

"Hello?" Dean called out, but got no response. "Looks like we're alone."

He dropped his backpack, kicked off his shoes, and made himself comfortable in the large fabric chair. I paced around the living room, as I let my eyes wander around. They quickly glanced at the new picture frame that held the old photograph of their father.

"What's your room like?" I asked curiously.

"That's right, you've never been upstairs," Dean commented, as he stroked his chin. "You wanna have a look?"

I followed Dean up the stairs, and into the first room on the right. It was darker than I imagined. The stone grey painted walls were covered with multiple band posters, and the one window in the corner was concealed behind a black shade. Clothes and books were scattered across the floor, and random items cluttered his shelves and tables. His shiny drum set, in the back right corner, took up the most space.

"Can you play for me?"

"Nah, you don't want to listen to me," Dean shook his head modestly.

I crossed my arms. "I played for you, remember? You owe me."

Dean raised his eyebrows, and smirked a little. "Touché, my friend, touché"

He went over to his bedside table, rummaged through his mess, and found two sets of earplugs. He handed the green pair to me, and then walked over to his drums.

"Ready?"

I sat on his bed and pushed the soft earplugs in. "Ready."

He twirled his drumsticks, then positioned himself. He started off softly, slowly, allowing a solid rhythm to take the lead. Each round, he'd add something more. So, it grew and grew, until it turned into an explosion of percussion. I watched as he pounded the beats out; his body flowing swiftly, his muscles flexing with the tempo, his face and eyes so concentrated on the music he played.

I felt my insides doing flips, and my heart racing, so I looked away. I leaned back on his bed, rested my head on his fluffy pillow that carried his scent, and closed my eyes as I enjoyed the tempo that coarsed through my body. I was so caught up in it, that I didn't even realize that it had stopped.

Before I knew it, Dean was laying on top of me. There was no need to open my eyes between the transition of the two. He kissed me, softly, slowly, just as he had played. And just like the drums, the rhythm grew and grew. His right hand sneaked under the line of my shirt, as it held onto my bare hip. It started traveling further, as it traced a line up and down my side.

Suddenly, the bedroom door swung open. "Hey Dean, have you seen my . . . good grief."

We quickly broke apart, and both turned a bright red.

"Alex," Dean panted. "Haven't you ever heard of knocking?"

Alex leaned against the frame of the door, with the most outraged look on his face. "Whatever, bro." He glared at me, then turned. "Exactly what I was afraid of . . ." he muttered to himself. Alex stormed away, slamming the door behind him.

Dean laid back on the bed, breathed heavily, and rubbed his face in distress. "Sorry about that."

"What's his problem?" I asked. "It's not like anything really happened."

Dean shook his head, and sat up on the edge of the bed. "It's a long story . . . don't worry about it."

I sighed from mental exhaustion. Just when we had taken one step forward, we had moved two steps back. It was always like that. I guess it would always be like that until the mystery was no more.

"I guess the mood has been killed," Dean mumbled, his back still turned to me.

"Kind of . . ." I replied, readjusting my shirt.

"I honestly didn't think he was coming home until later."

I crinkled my eyebrows and paused. What exactly did he think was going to happen?

"Would it have made a difference?"

He turned to me, his dark hair still messy. "I don't know, you tell me."

Just as I had suspected. He thought we would go all the way. "Dean, I don't think I'm ready for that. I mean . . . what were you thinking? We've only been together for a few weeks."

"I don't know," he stammered. "I mean we've never talked about it or anything. How was I supposed to know? I thought maybe you had done it with Blake or something."

I shook my head. "Have you . . . done it?"

This time, he shook his head. "I've been waiting for the right girl," he answered softly.

I curled my arms around his back, and kissed the back of his next. "Look, I just don't think I'm ready for that quite yet."

"Okay, when you're ready then," he whispered, with a nod.

I felt kind of bad, because he was ready and I wasn't. "And you don't mind waiting?"

He let out a light chuckle. "I've waited this long, haven't I?" He turned and kissed my nose. "When you're ready . . . no pressure. Even if it takes weeks, months, years! I don't care, I can wait forever for you. Just tell me when."

I didn't quite frankly know when I would be. When I was with Blake, I had always wanted to wait until I was married. Although I felt a hell of a lot stronger for Dean, I still couldn't tell if he was the one I wanted to lose it to. We still had our problems, and at times, he still felt like a stranger. Once you lose it, it's gone forever.

I wanted to be absolutely sure that it was with the right guy, and it was too early to tell if Dean was the one.

"Thank you for understanding," I whispered, before giving him a light peck.

"Really, it's no problem. I never want you to ever feel uncomfortable," he replied. "Should I take you home now?"

I shook my head. "Not yet." I laid down and pulled him down next to me. He wrapped his arms around me, and just held me. "Just a few more minutes."

CHapTer 25

And so, the court date countdown began. We worked harder, we worked longer, we worked until we could work no more.

When the holiday season rolled around, we gratefully took the break. All three of us knew that when we regrouped in January, there wouldn't be a second to waste. We were going to have to go above and beyond if we wanted to win. We needed more research, more background information, more evidence . . . anything that would help our case.

When school started back up again, Dean and I fell into a natural routine: meet in the morning, survive the school day, go to my house and work with my father until the night was over, and repeat.

Dean and I became so consumed by this lawsuit that our grades fell to the wayside. It was a hard price to pay, but worth it. My father had difficulty focusing on his other clients, but did his best to balance all of his cases as long as he could.

It was just days before the court date that Dean unexpectantly broke our daily cycle. It was Thursday of that monumental week that I had to take the bus and walked to Chemisty by myself. I wondered about his whereabouts with rage. Dean better come up with some damn good excuse. He knew that we were going to be in the court room on Saturday. He knew how crucial these last few days were.

On the bright side, this gave me a chance to approach Lucy for the first time in weeks. Along with my grades, my friendship with her had suffered because of this.

"Hey Lucy," I called out to her, as our class shuffled out of the room. "Wait up!"

But she didn't wait, didn't stop, didn't even bear to slow down. I huffed, then picked up my pace, and pushed through the crowd until I was by her side.

"Lucy. Hey," I caught my breath, waiting for her response. "How are you?"

She sneered, and avoided my eyes. "Oh, so now you talk to me?" In an attempt to get away from me, she took longer, faster strides. "Now that your boyfriend isn't here, you're lonely and come running back?"

"Are you mad?" I inquired, confused. "I thought you'd understand."

"Yeah, my best friend has ditched and snubbed me for her new boyfriend," she spat. Then said sarcastically, "I totally understand." She gritted her teeth, and turned sharply down the corner of the hall. I struggled to keep up with her. "You know, even when you were Blake, even when he tried to take up all your time, you still made an effort for me. Now, it's like you don't even care."

She was jealous . . . and hurt. I probably would have been too, but she had it all wrong.

I sighed. "I know Lucy, I've been really busy and I know that's not an excuse but I've had a lot going on," I tried to explain.

"I don't know anything about what's going on, Riley, because you haven't told me," she snapped loudly, stopping in the dead middle of the hall. "The only person you speak to these days is Dean. I mean, seriously! What's the point of having a best friend if you're always going to pick your boyfriend. What's the point of having both if you can't manage to balance the two . . ." she started to step away from me. "Think about that, and give me a call when you're ready to actually be my best friend again, and not a ghost."

I didn't bother to try and follow her. I let her go, just as I had let my most important friendship go. She was right. Every word she said was true. But how could I juggle all of this? A lawsuit, a mysterious boyfriend, a dysfunctional family, a needy best friend, an abusive ex, and on top of that, school. It was too much for seventeen-year-old to manage. I couldn't do it all. I could only focus and succeed on the most important factors in my life right now. Atleast until some of them were resolved.

I sat alone at the lunch table that day. It was the first time in weeks that I had actually done something alone. I had no stepping stone, no person to depend on. Just me, myself, and I. And as I ate my macaroni salad by myself, I came to realize that I was too dependent on everybody else. In breaking out of my relationship with Blake, I had hoped to gain some independence. I told myself I would take baby steps. I had done just the opposite. Instead, I had leeched onto and survived off of somebody else. Three somebody elses to be exact. And now at school, with no father, no boyfriend, no best friend, I had to fend for my own. And that's exactly what I learned to do that day in the lunch room.

For the first time in months, I survived an intervention with Blake on my own. A brief intervention, but an intervention none the less.

He sat down at my empty table, and waited for me to say something like "What do you want Blake?" or "Leave me alone."

But I stared down at my food, and ate in silence. Eventually, he gave in.

"What, no security guards today?"

I dabbed my mouth with my napkin and looked up at him. "What, no motley crew today?"

"You know," he bent over, cranking his head closer to mine. "When it comes down to it, in the end, it's just you and me."

I smirked at his sorry attempt to intimidate me. "You and me and the devil makes three," I smartly replied, with an eyebrow raise.

He peered at me, with those harsh, piercing ocean eyes. "You think you're clever, don't you?"

"I know I am," I shrugged, shoving a forkful of food into my mouth.

He crossed his arms. "I hope you're bringing your A-game on Saturday. You don't want to seem entirely pathetic when you lose. Then you can at least say you put up a fair fight."

"You know, I'm going to laugh when I see that shocked expression on your face when the jury proves you guilty," I cocked my head at him, and stared him dead in the face.

"We'll see who's laughing in the end," he spat, as he got up from the table. He took a few steps away, then turned back around. "Oh, and tell your little Ponyboy I'll see him later tonight."

He left me baffled by his words. What did he mean by that, and what was going on? Dean has some serious explaining to do.

After a long, lonesome day at school, I finally made it home. I crawled up to my father's office, threw my backpack on the floor, and slumped in one of his chairs. My father was diligently working, scribbling on some documents.

"Where's Dean?" He asked, putting down his fountain pen.

"Don't know . . . he didn't show up today," I muttered.

My father looked disheartened and disappointed, but suppressed his emotions as lawyers always do. They work with their heads, not their hearts.

"No worries, we can work without him," my father replied, handing me a stack of papers.

So we got cracking away. Obviously, three pairs of hands is better than two, so we weren't at our usual pace. Nonetheless, we worked well and got some good one-on-one bonding time. Without Dean as a buffer, we were able to chat about father-daughter stuff.

Around 5:30, the door bell rang. My mother, who had just gotten home answered it, then called for me.

"Riley, your juvenile delinquent wants to see you," she snarled, as she fetched me from my father's study. She obviously was still not used to the idea of having Dean around regularly. When he was over helping us, she tried her best to avoid him with bare minimal interaction.

I approached the door, and made sure I had a fowl expression on my face. "Dean . . ." I got one good look at him, and dropped my mouth. He looked terrible. His eyes were red and tired, his clothes were wrinkled, and his hair was out of control. "What's going on? Where were you today? Blake mentioned something about you too."

"Blake?" He raised his eyebrows. "Look, Riley, I'm sorry, I can explain, but we don't have much time." He took my hand and started pulling me towards his motorcycle.

"Dean, wait," I broke loose. "What do you mean we don't have time? Where are we going?"

"Riley, we have to go," Dean sounded panicked and desperate. "I need to show you, I need to explain before it's too late. Just please, come with me."

I sighed. I couldn't ignore a desperate cry for help. So I strapped onto the back of his bike, and we took off.

CHAPTER 26

"**W**here are we?"

"Foreman's Factory's Garage," Dean answered, walking towards the dark abyss. "It closed down years ago."

"Cool," I whispered.

Dean sat in one of the empty parking spots, with the number 58 labeled on it, so I sat down next to him. I didn't dare ask why we were here, but Dean seemed to read my mind.

"This is where my father used to work . . . before it closed down," he paused. "And this is where he died."

I held my breath in my lungs. This was the truth, the whole truth, nothing but the truth. No more questions, assumptions, or conclusions to be made.

"Shit, I'm so sorry Dean," I sympathized, because I didn't know what else to say.

Dean shivered slightly. "It's okay. It was a long ago, but it still really hurts."

"I'm so sorry," I repeated, lightly massaging his shoulder.

"Alex doesn't want me telling you this, but you deserve to know," he croaked. "My father was one of founders of the gang my brother and I are currently in. He led the Black Knights a really long time, up until I was the age of thirteen. But he became distracted, and started to focus more on other aspects of his life. And that became his downfall. He received threats from rival gangs about some risky business the gang had been involved in, but he didn't pay close enough attention, until it was too late . . . they came here one night, and waited in the shadows of this very parking spot. He didn't know. Just as he was about to approach his car, they shot him dead."

"Oh God . . ." I whimpered, hit with the weight of the world. And one by one, the cracks in the wall between us started to grow, causing the structure to crumble.

"My brother took over, and I joined the gang as well. At the time, I didn't mind the trouble it caused me. It felt good to be . . . reckless, and I was able to channel my anger through it. But after I met you, I didn't feel as though it was worth it anymore. I didn't need the low life bums I called my brothers . . . I just needed you. And that's why my brother hates you."

I crinkled my eyebrows, trying to process all of this at one time. My head was spinning because of everything I had just learned, but somehow I felt closer to Dean.

"Because . . . I stole you away from him?"

Dean shook his head. "No, no that's not it at all! He's afraid I'm going to follow in my father's path. He's afraid that you'll be a distraction, and I'll become careless and well . . . you know, lose myself. Especially now, when Blake and his buddies are provoking us."

I took deep gulps of air, trying to steady my breathing. I pulled my knees to my chest, and wrapped my arms in a cradle. Too much was hitting me at once. The tragedy of his father's death, the drive for his brother's hate.

"Can't you leave the gang?" I asked, indicating to the solution of all of Dean's problems.

"Technically, I could. But too much of my life has been absorbed into it. Once a Black Knight, always a Black Knight," Dean mumbled, before taking my hands. "Look, Riley, I know this is a lot and I don't expect you to understand. I just . . . I couldn't leave tonight without you knowing everything."

I looked up at him with trembling, frazzled eyes. He looked so strong, so focused, so determined. He pulled me in closely to him, in an attempt to comfort me through all of this.

"Where are you going?" I inquired, my voice shaking.

"There's a fight tonight. Between us and them," he lowly stated, with an unbearable tone of seriousness.

"A fight?" The pitch of my voice raised, as I pondered.

Dean sighed. "I don't want you to worry though."

I bit my bottom lip. "Okay."

Dean stood up, and offered me his hand. After I pulled myself to my feet, Dean slung his arm around me and led us to his motorcycle.

As we drove to his house, I was finally able to gather my thoughts and breathe. We finally arrived, and walked into his warm, heated home.

"Where is everyone?" I asked, taking off the leather jacket Dean had given me for my birthday. I was wearing it more and more every day, and it had become a part of me, like Dean had.

"Mom's got the graveyard shift. Alex is out, getting ready for tonight," Dean paused. "I'm meeting up with him later."

He nudged me to follow him up the stairs. We locked ourselves in his bedroom, and sat quietly on the edge of his bed. He kept taking deep, burly breaths. I rubbed his back with my hands, and briefly kissed his ear.

"I want you to know that if anything happens to me . . . I love you."

Those three little words echoed in my ears. I had never heard them said before so honestly, so truthfully. After being cut down so much by Blake, I believed for so long that I wasn't worthy of love.

I blinked a few times, making sure I had heard him correctly. "You . . . love me?" I blinked some more in awe.

Dean nervously smiled. "Yeah." His smile faded. "I mean . . . it's early, but I've felt like this for a while. It's okay if you don't love me, at least not --"

"I love you too, Dean," I found myself saying. The words slipped out without any thought. I didn't need to think twice about it. I meant it.

I can't tell you what love is. That's just because I don't know.

But whatever it was, I felt for Dean. Why? I couldn't tell you. May it be his undying support for me, his charisma and charm, or his protective and passionate nature? Who knows?

I never wanted to spend every minute with anyone else. I never wanted to let him go. That's how I knew I loved him, even if I didn't fully understand the meaning of love itself.

The wall had fallen. The barrier was gone. The mystery of Dean Marks had been solved.

Just me and him.

Dean proceeded to kiss me, softly seducing me with his passionate lips. I wrapped my arms and legs around him, pulling him closer, eager to feel his embrace even more. I leaned back and let him caress me with his hands and mouth.

I broke away in a moment of panic. "You're brother's not going to barge in again, is he?"

Dean let out a gentle laugh. "No, he's not," he grinned, kissing me again.

I laid back with him, hoping he would read my body language. Together, as one, we slid up on his bed, until my head was resting on his pillow. I kissed him with more fire and lust than before. He continued to kiss me, but nothing more. I was going to have to be blunt with him.

"Dean," I whispered between a breath.

"Yeah?"

I looked up at him, and stared into his sparkling midnight eyes. "I'm ready."

He crinkled his nose. "For?" I raised an eyebrow at him, and winked. "Oh. Now?"

"Is that okay?"

He kissed me instead of answering. I lifted his shirt over his head, revealing his toned upper body. He did the same for me. And from there, it all became instinctual.

Reaching over to his bedside table, he grabbed a condom and began to unwrap it. I worked on loosening the buckle of his belt looped through his jeans. We began to undress each other, until it was just our bare bodies pressed against each other.

He kissed me softly, deeply and held me close. After he put the condom on, he moved his lower body towards mine. I looked up at him, with tender eyes. I gave him a small nod and let him know it was okay to proceed.

At first, all I felt was pain. Everywhere. He fought his way through, pushing gently but firmly into me. He held onto me tightly, kissing my face everywhere, trying to ease the pain. Then, I felt something happen, and suddenly he was in.

He began to thrust harder, faster, deeper. Our bodies became one as we created a rhythm of motion. Before I knew it, the pain was concealed with pleasure.

And I was in complete bliss.

"So you'll call so I know you're okay, right?" I handed him my helmet as I got off.

Dean smoothed down my hair. "Yes, the moment I can." He paused to kiss me. "How are you feeling? I hope I didn't hurt you too much."

"It was going to hurt no matter what," I sighed. "But it got better as it went on"

He flashed me his crooked smile. "I love you so much, Riley."

"I love you too," I grinned, brushing my nose against his. "Be safe, okay?" I stepped away from him.

He strapped on his dark helmet, concealing his face. "I promise."

I gave him a meek wave, and traveled up my driveway. He zipped up his leather jacket, made some noise, and drove off. I held onto the doorknob of my front door and took a deep breath. I had just lost my virginity to a guy who I may possibly never see again.

My father and I spent the remainder of the night glued to the phone. He absolutely didn't support the idea of Dean partaking in a gang fight because it could only add unnecessary weight to the lawsuit, but he was just as nervous yet hopeful as I was. We sat there in silence all night, staring at the phone, waiting for the LCD screen to light up and the ringer to explode.

The minutes, the hours dragged on. And with the more time that passed, the more nervous we became. How long could a rumble possibly take?

It was the early hours of the morning, much before dawn, when the phone rang, waking both my father and I from our dreadful sleep in his office chairs.

"Hullo? Dean?" Despite my grogginess, I became frantic as I put him on speakerphone.

"Riley, please, you have to come to the hospital," he begged with desperation and pain which broke my heart. My mind was racing with possibilities, and uneasy feeling rested in the pit of my stomach. I could only assume the worst.

My father pipped in. "Son, what's wrong? What happened?"

Dean whimpered. "It's Alex . . ."

CHAPTER 27

My father and I rushed down to the hospital as soon as we hung up. Dean, traumatized by whatever had happened, wasn't able to say much. Although Alex and I had our differences, Dean needed me, so I was going to have to push my selfish rivalries aside.

We arrived in a timely matter. The streets were practically empty at this hour of the night, so exceeding the speed limit by thirty-five miles per hour was not an issue. Besides, this was an emergency.

We marched through the hospital, eagerly seeking the ER. When we got to the right floor, my father boldly approached the nurse behind the desk.

"Hello, I'm looking for Alex Marks?"

"Family?"

"No . . ." he paused. "But it's very crucial that I see him immediately."

The nurse shook her head. "I'm sorry sir, but I can't allow that. Hospital policy. You're just going to have to wait."

My father grunted and I followed him to the waiting room, where we nervously sat in uncomfortable blue leather chairs.

We sat in silence like we had all night, waiting for the phone. This time, we were unable to drift into sleep because we knew something was wrong. One by one we watched as people waiting in agony like us were escorted to their victim's room. We still lingered behind all the rest.

Just as we were becoming restless to the point of insanity, Dean popped out. His hair was unbearably messy, his clothes were covered in dirt and blood, and he wore a long, tired, bruised face.

I jumped to my feet and ran over to him, throwing my arms around him. He winced a little, but held the embrace.

I took his bloody face in my hands. "I'm so glad you're alright."

"Riley . . . Alex . . ." he stammered. "He's really hurt."

My father caught up to us. "Son, what happened? Where is he?"

"They moved him to Intensive Care," Dean mumbled. "They weren't going to until they had a room ready, but Mom insisted."

"Can we see him?" I asked.

Dean nodded, and led the way. We followed him through the sterile hallways. Automatic beeps from monitors echoed from the white rooms. Nurses bustled from room to room. Patients on stretchers were pushed passed us by large teams.

"Well . . . room 103."

None of us wanted to step in. None of us wanted to see the cruel reality that laid before us. Dean and I lingered by the door frame, while my father was brave enough to step in. I watched and studied his expression, cold and serious, as it always was whenever he needed to control his emotions.

I peeked in, only to see Alex torn to pieces, coated in a thin layer of blood. I had to look away.

"What's . . . what's wrong with him?" I nervously asked.

Dean sighed. "Too much. He's got internal bleeding and he's lost so much blood. But . . . that's . . ." he stopped, unable to continue.

He slid down the wall, and cried. To see a man cry is a strange yet beautiful thing. There were no sobs, no hysterics, no blubbering. Just a composure of soft weeps and meek tears. I sat down next to him, and threw my arms around him. He had been through too much in one day.

"It's okay, Dean . . ." I cooed, rubbing his back.

He sniffled. "Blake . . . he was coming after me . . . Alex protected me, he . . . came between us. And Blake . . . stabbed him, right . . . right square in the chest . . . it's too deep . . . they don't know if they can stitch him up or . . . stop the bleeding."

My eyes widened; I couldn't believe what I was hearing.

"He said . . . 'Dad had something to live for . . . his family . . . you have something to live for . . . you could do something with your life . . . and me . . . well I'm nothing . . .'" he paused, and looked at me with tear filled eyes. "I can't lose him . . . I can't . . . Mom needs him . . . I need him."

He pulled me close, and pressed his face into my chest. I stroked his hair with my fingers.

"You won't lose him, Dean, you won't," I whispered, holding him close.

He composed himself, and asked,"How do you know?"

I paused. How did I know? I wasn't a doctor, I couldn't determine if he would live or die. How did I know?

"Because . . ." I started. "He'll always be with you. Just like your father is always with you."

We held onto each other, knowing that we only had each other. Knowing that together, we would get through this, through anything.

"Dean, your mother wants to see you," my father murmured, as he came out of the room.

Dean nodded, lifted his tired eyes, stood up and walked in to the room where his dying brother laid. My father watched him with sorry, sympathetic eyes, then turned to me.

"He's in bad shape . . ."

I nodded and bit on my lip. "I know . . . hey, Dad?"

He raised his eyebrows. "Yes?"

"Blake did it."

My father lowered his eyes at me. "Did this to Alex?"

I slowly nodded, unveiling the truth that stared us in the face.

"How's our case looking now?"

"Well . . ." he stopped to think deeply. "The charges continue to stack up. Gang violence, assault and battery, and if Alex passes, God forbid, second degree murder."

"Wow," I huffed.

"But Dean . . . "

I cocked my head at him. "What about him?"

"Well, if we put him on the stand as a witness, he could be charged for gang violence, and then we would have another court case to deal with."

"Is that avoidable?"

He shook his head. "It could go either way," he whispered.

I let out a heavy sigh. "Is it worth the risk?"

"Absolutely," my father nodded. "It's up to Dean though, if he's willing to take that risk for you. We could get by without him as a witness, but it'd be a lot harder to win."

I sighed. Even if Dean did agree, I wouldn't want him to destroy his life for me. As his brother said, he could do something with his life; go to college, get a successful job. But how would it look if he had a criminal record? How much harder would it be for him to get somewhere in life? I couldn't let him throw that all away for me.

"I don't know, Dad . . . I'd feel awful," I murmured. "And I couldn't imagine asking him for such a big favor right now, with all that has happened."

"Look, we can go into the lawsuit without him . . . we can see how it's going, and then if we need to, we can ask and see what he says. How's that?"

I nodded. "I'm going to go in, okay?"

Pulling myself to my feet, I took a deep breath and entered the room. Dean was sitting beside his brother, holding his limp hand, while his mother hovered over her two sons in misery. I stared at this family, flawed but full of love.

A gang family, with a father dead, and a son dying. But a family nonetheless, who loved and stood by each other. A family who could not be destroyed, but only defeated.

Mrs. Marks came over to and hugged me. "Thank you for coming."

"I'm so sorry . . . about everything."

Her glassy eyes shimmered in the fluorescent light. "Not to worry, dear. Please, just take my son home and make sure he gets some rest. I'm going to spend the rest of the night here."

"Are you sure you want to stay?"

"Yes, of course. I can't leave Alex's side," she murmured. "Just take Dean home with you. It's been a rough day for him."

"Okay," I meekly smiled.

She let go, went over to Dean, and whispered to him about what was happening. He kissed her goodbye, kissed his motionless brother goodbye, and followed us out to the parking lot. My father and I crawled into our car as Dean hopped onto his motorcycle. When all three of us were back home, we all quietly returned into my father's study.

"So, considering the late hour, I think it's best you two stay home tomorrow and rest."

"Thank you Mr. Jennings for letting me stay the night," Dean cooed, his voice weak from exhaustion and depression.

"Our door is always open to you, son. You're practically family to us now," he grinned. "Just . . . don't let Mrs. Jennings know that you're here," he added, contradicting himself. "You can sleep in Riley's room . . . given the circumstances, I think I can make an exception this one time."

"Understood, sir," Dean replied, heading towards my bedroom door. "Goodnight sir."

"Goodnight," my father echoed. "Goodnight, Riley."

"Goodnight, Dad," I called before following Dean into my bedroom.

Dean and I didn't speak much after that. We didn't necessarily sleep either. It was hard to after all the excitement we had experienced in one day. So we just laid silently in my bed, looked at my glow-in-the-dark stars, and enjoyed each other's quiet company.

CHAPTER 28

Day One of Trial

Alex Frank Marks died three days later. The doctors tried what they could, but they were unable to stop the flow of blood to his chest. Blood transfusions were just not enough to keep him alive. The funeral was the day before our court date. After a touching, emotional ceremony, the three of us were more blood thirsty for revenge than ever before.

"I'm going to make sure Blake pays for this, for all of this," Dean had whispered to me as they had lowered his brother into the ground. "If it's the last thing I do."

Now, as I dressed in my blouse and pencil skirt for my court appearance, I thought of Alex who was looking down upon us, giving his blessing. I stared at myself in the mirror, studying every inch of my face. I didn't look much different, but I felt different. It had been a long journey, and I had come to the end of it as a changed person. I no longer lived within a shell, within a stereotype, but now lived on my own accord.

There was a knock at the door.

"Come in," I called, putting down my hairbrush.

My mother, who I had avoided for the past few weeks, came in and sat on my bed. She was still in her sleeping attire; fuzzy pajamas and curlers.

"How are you feeling?"

I made eye contact with her in the mirror. "Nervous."

She nodded. "It's normal to be. I just want you to know that . . . whatever happens, I'm proud of you."

I smiled meekly. Although it wasn't much, her words had touched me. Our relationship had never been loving or tender, so just to hear her say that was a big step for us.

I turned to face her. "Thanks Mom."

"Be strong, okay?"

"I always am," I replied, tucking a lock of hair behind my ear.

"I know you are," she beamed. "You always have been." She paused, and looked at me with glimmering eyes. "Well, I better let you get ready."

I bit down on my bottom lip. "Okay," I replied as she went out the door.

Flopping onto my bed, I tried to calm the butterflies that rested in the pit of my stomach. This was really happening, the day I had waited so long for was finally here. It was overly exciting yet terribly frightening.

My father beckoned me to the car, causing my emotions to stir. The hour long car ride proved to be a nightmare, as it appeared that we couldn't get there fast enough. By the time we did actually arrive, I felt like I was going to explode. Dean was promptly early, waiting for us in the parking lot. Dressed in a casual suit, he looked even better cleaned up. I hopped out of the car, and walked towards him, letting him plant one on me right in front of my father.

"Are you ready?" He quietly asked. He had been such a good sport through all of this. He stood before me with an encouraging grin on his face when his close brother had just died days before. I would never quite understand how he was able to pull himself together for me.

I sighed. "More than ever."

"You're going to be great, I know it," he exclaimed, kissing me again.

"I hope so."

With my loyal boyfriend and supportive father by my side, I was ready to tackle this lawsuit head on. Together, all three of us marched into the court house, proud, determined, and strong. The high ceiling above us and the light that beamed through the stained glass windows gave us hope for a brighter day. As soon as the doors opened, we hurried to our seats. My father and I on one side, with Dean sitting directly behind us in the audience.

Blake, his broad father, and a gimpy looking attorney in a wrinkled suit entered moments after us. We stood up as they approached, taking their sweet, glorified time. Blake's team looked equally as confident as us.

Blake, dressed and tamed, stepped towards me. "Good luck," he sneered, extending his hand out to me. "You'll need it."

"Same to you," I said, gripping his hand. He squeezed as hard as he could, crushing the bones down to the cartilage in my hand, trying to faze me. "It's going to take a lot more than that," I hissed, squeezing with great force.

He winced, and let go. Blake glared at us with fiery eyes before taking his seat. His father and the attorney nodded in acknowledgment, then proceeded to take their seats as well. The jury entered, followed by the bailiff. He approached both sides of the room, swearing each of us under oath.

"All rise for the Honorable Judge White," he announced, causing us all to rise to our feet.

An elder looking man dressed in black robes entered from the back room. He climbed up his stairs, into his box seat that peered upon us.

"Case 274, Jennings versus Salato. Parties have been sworn in, you may be seated," the bailiff commanded.

"Mr. Jennings, this is your daughter?" Judge White asked.

"Yes, your honor," he answered, nodding.

"According to the file, you wish to sue upon charges of domestic violence, following under assault, battery, harassment, and attempted sexual assault. Is all of the following correct?"

"Yes, your honor."

"Please expand on the preexisting relationship of these two young minors," the judge ordered.

"Ms. Jennings and Mr. Salato began dating about a year back, around mid summer of last year. Like any typical high school relationship, they had their issues, but nothing appeared be out of the ordinary. A few months in, Ms. Jennings began to act differently. She was vague, distant, depressed, and sensitive about certain issues. After that, we began to notice bruises and cuts up and down her body. She finally confessed that Mr. Salato had lost his temper and had given her these injuries."

"Does the defendant testify against these allegations?" Judge White turned to Blake's side.

The meek lawyer stood up. "Your honor, my defendant does not deny these accusation but simply testifies that the plaintiff's statements are exaggerated."

The judge stroked his chin, deeply considering everything that had been presented. "I see, what proposal do you have to make?"

"We suggest a standard restraining order between the defendant and plaintiff, your honor," the lawyer informed.

Trying to remain respectful, I fought the urge to roll my eyes. We all knew that wasn't going to do anything . . .

"Continue."

My father and Blake's attorney had at it for a while, spitting out judicial terms and phrases, trying to sell their case to the jury.

Much after they were tired out by logistics, I was called to the stand. This was it; my moment to shine.

"Ms. Jennings, how long were you with Mr. Salato?" The attorney asked.

I paused and counted the months on my fingers. "Close to six months."

"And how long had these assaults been going on?"

"I'd say about four months."

He turned to the jury, then back at me. "So you're telling me that you endured such brutality for four months?"

"That would be correct," I murmured.

"What I don't seem to understand is . . . why would you let something like that go on for so long? You must have wanted to put it to an end at the beginning. Why not escape the defendant when it was easier to leave rather than later when his hooks were in you even more? Obviously, it must have not been that bad or else why would you put yourself through all of that?"

I looked up at the judge, with pleading eyes. "Which should I answer first?"

"Objection," my father called out. "Irrelevant."

"Denied," the judge replied before turning to me. "Ms. Jennings, answer the questions."

I looked over at Dean, who gave me a nod of reassurance. "Like any abusive relationship, the interventions start out small. I kept telling myself over and over again that he was just acting up, had a bad day, and everything would go back to normal. But with time, it only gradually became worse. I was living in denial for most of the relationship, afraid to really say that I was being abused. And by the time I snapped into reality, it was too late. I had tried to end the relationship, but Blake wouldn't have it."

The jury bursted into whispers, as they analyzed what I had just said.

"Exactly how severe were your injuries? Did you ever have to go to the hospital?"

I felt a bead of sweat form at the top of my forehead. "I never had to seek medical treatment, but I thought they were bad enough. I still have some scars if you'd like to see proof."

The attorney turned to the judge. "Objection. Scars cannot be used as viable evidence. How are we supposed to know if the plaintiff got an identifiable scar from the defendant or an accident falling off her bicycle."

"Sustained."

"Your honor," my father stood up. "We do have viable evidence that will help our case."

My father handed the video tape to the bailiff, who delivered it to the judge. He examined it, then handed it back to the bailiff, with orders to play it for the room to see. After pulling out the video player and dimming the lights, the room turned its focus to the projection screen. I couldn't bear to watch that again, so I focused on a loose thread on my skirt. Gasps spread across the whole room as they watched me get beaten to shreds.

When the lights came back on, the entire room was in discussion, clamoring about such horror and filth.

The judge banged his gavel. "Order . . . order!"

"Your honor, the lighting and quality of that security tape is far too indistinct. How can we attest to that really being the defendant and plaintiff?"

"Who else would it be? Do you think I staged that?" I exclaimed, bouncing out of my seat. I couldn't stand by and have somebody tell me that wasn't authentic. This entire case rested on that video tape. Without it, we had nothing. After realizing my outburst, I pulled back and sat in silence.

"No further questions," the attorney announced, buttoning his suit jacket.

The jury gossiped, evaluating his legitimate point and my outburst. I sighed, and returned to my seat. We were going to lose, we had nothing. We had been foolish to think that our entire case could depend on a skeptical security video tape. We had been foolish to not have made a Plan B.

"I've heard enough for the day," the judge proclaimed, banging his gavel. "This court will resume session tomorrow at 11 AM."

Everyone except the jury exited the court room, filing into the hallways. Dean came over and gave me a much needed hug, while my father dragged me aside.

"I'm so sorry, Dad," I cried, as we gathered in a corner. "I just don't know what came over me."

"We've got do something, and fast," my father ordered. "We've got to come up with something else by tomorrow or else we should just throw in the towel now."

"I'll go on the stand tomorrow," Dean offered proudly.

My mouth dropped. "No, Dean, you can't. I won't let you. Think about your future."

"Riley, I want you to win, and if that means going on the stand, then I'll do it," he purred. "You know I'd do anything for you."

My father looked like he was about to agree, when suddenly his face twisted. "Actually . . . I think we can do this a different way."

Day Two of Trial

"We'd like to call defendant Blake Salato to the stand," my father requested at the start of our next day in court.

Blake grinned, slicked back his hair and approached the bench.

"Mr. Salato, you don't deny hitting my Ms. Jennings, correct?"

"Yes sir. I may have lost my temper and done something foolish in the heat of the moment, but it was never very severe. I never meant to harm her."

"But you did cause damage to her?"

"No, but I think the way she processed it had a stronger effect, leaving her to think that it was much worse than it really was," he replied. "You know, all relationships have their issues. It all depends on how a person will react to those problems."

My father lifted and eyebrow. "So you're saying that my daughter has been lying this entire time and has nothing to be traumatized by?"

"Not exactly . . . I admit I've made some mistakes, but I've learned from them. I deserve only a fair punishment, right?"

The jury murmured in response. His wording was perfectly precise, to say just the right thing. Clearly, he had been practicing what to say. I only hoped that the rest of the jury saw how rehearsed he was.

"Mr. Salato, have you had other anger issues?"

"I play football. It's natural for football players to be physical and aggressive," Blake calmly answered.

"But have you ever violently struck a person, excluding the plaintiff?"

"Well . . . sure," Blake paused, carefully plotting his answer. "My friends and I like to fight and fool around sometimes. You know how boys can be."

The court room whispered some more, obviously in agreement.

"Harmless, you say? So let's define harmless a bit more for the jury. Let's say play fighting, a little wrestling here and there. Am I on the right track?"

Blake nodded.

My father continued. "Boys will be boys, right? So to elaborate, this sort of casual fighting you do, it's totally safe and nobody gets hurt, right? For instance, you've never had to send somebody to the hospital from your harmless fighting, correct?"

Blake was cracking under the pressure; he knew we were onto him. His eyes darted back and forth, from the jury to his father to Dean and me. Clearly, he wasn't expecting this and hadn't been coached on the matter. I wondered if he had even told his lawyer or his father about the fight he participated in against the Black Knights. He leaned back in his chair, and tried to look casual.

"None . . . none of my friends have ever been sent to the hospital . . . at least in regards to our childish fights."

"None of your friends? How about somebody who's not your friend?"

Blake nervously smirked, becoming short of breath. "I'm not sure I know what you're asking."

My father turned to the jury and launched into story time:

"When I was a kid, growing up in the late fifties and mid sixties, my friends and I used to like to fight like Blake and his buds do. We were called, Greasers. You know, slicked back hair, leather jackets, tight blue jeans. After a while, we got tired of fighting each other and wanted something fresh. That's when we started fighting other groups of guys and had friendly competitions. We used to think we were so clever and cool," my dad cooed, slicking back his head. "Who knew I'd turn into this old man, am I right?"

The jury let out a little laugh, obviously entertained by my father's story.

"Although all this time has passed, some things never change, such as a young man's desire to fight," my father turned to Blake. "Are you telling me that you and your pals have never fought other group of guys?"

"No . . . well, I mean, we might have once or twice," Blake stuttered. A bead of sweat formed on his crinkled forehead.

"Anything recently? Say in the last week or so?"

"Um . . . I don't think so."

Blake's eyes darted, as he nervously glanced around the room. My father was onto something, and both Blake and the rest of the courtroom knew it.

"Fuzzy memory? Are you on any kind of drugs that could possibly handicap your memory?"

He gulped, and loosened the tie around his neck. "No . . . no sir."

"Do you remember about hearing about a big fight down at Waterfront Park this past Tuesday?"

Blake shook his head frantically.

"You didn't? Well that's surprising, seeing how your best friend, Parker Lee, was found at the site of the fight and had to be rushed to the hospital. That doesn't sound very harmless, now does it."

Blake was sweating like a pig, shifting nervously in his seat, and biting down on his lip. "I wasn't there, if that's what you're asking."

My father kept going, his voice becoming louder, his questions more direct. "Right right, you already made that clear but are you sure he didn't tell you? Considering how close you two must be to consider each other best pals."

Blake shook his head once more.

"Well then, you must have at least heard that a young man, by the name of Alex Marks, was killed in this fight. Surely, you must have, seeing how you must be in the loop of all of current crime news because of your father. So, you're telling me you know absolutely nothing about all of this? Doesn't that sound a bit suspicious to you?"

"Uh . . . um . . . I don't know what you're talking about sir," Blake stammered, with tears in his eyes.

"Objection, your honor," Blake's lawyer called out. "How is this relevant?"

"Rejected," the judge replied. "But I do agree, answer the questions Mr. Salato, then get on with your point Mr. Jennings."

My father nodded, and looked back at Blake who was tugging on the collar of his button down.

"I heard about it . . . the fight. And I know Parker got hurt . . . but I didn't know that Alex Marks was dead . . ." Tears flooded to his eyes, overwhelmed with the news.

My father was unsure how to proceed. I could see that in his eyes as he stroked his chin. "No further questions," my father announced, before going up to the judges podium. He whispered a few words to the judge, and the judge nodded in agreement.

"This hearing will reconvene in thirty minutes," he proclaimed, before banging the gavel.

The judge disappeared into his backroom, as my father came back for his folders. He pointed for Dean to come join him.

"Dad, what did you just say to him? What's going on?"

My father narrowed his eyes down at me. "This is not going how I wanted it to go. But there is something I can still do to keep you safe, and end this nightmare once and for all. As long as I have Dean's permission."

"Sure, what's up Mr. Jennings?" Dean asked, looking at me then back at my father.

"I want to change this from assault trial..." my father lowered his voice. "To a murder trial."

Both of our mouths dropped.

"But, Dad?" I shrieked.

My father raised his hand. "Look Riley, the best we will get out of this is a restraining order. Trust me, but those don't last, and psychos like Blake don't abide to them. Now Blake has committed a serious crime, and could face at least a second-degree murder charge. He could be locked up for twenty five to fifty years."

"So let's do it," I exclaimed, without a beat.

My father rubbed his eyes, and I turned to look at Dean, who was still in shock. "Well, while you would no longer be involved . . . Dean would."

Dean looked at the ground, appearing to be in his own world. I wondered if he had heard anything my father had just said. Suddenly, he snapped out of it and looked at us.

"Let's do it."

My father sighed. "Are you absolutely sure? You know that as his brother, you would be the plaintiff in this trial."

Dean slowly nodded. "I need to do this. For Alex. To protect his name and preserve his memory. He meant a great deal to me. I know you didn't know him well, Riley, and I know you didn't know him at all Mr. Jennings, but he was truly a great man. He would have wanted us to fight for his name, and he would have wanted to see a scumbag like Blake behind bars. Only the good die young. People like my brother don't deserve to die, and people like Blake don't deserve to live . . . at least not freely."

My heart melted for Dean. His words of passion showed me that he really wanted to do this; not just for me, not just for his brother, but even for himself.

"But Dad, what will happen to Dean?" I asked. "Won't he get in trouble for gang violence?"

"Well, because Dean is stepping up and reporting a much larger crime, he won't be charged. It's a little legal protection we offer so we can catch the real bad guys."

"Then I'm in," Dean answered, looking deeply into my eyes. "I'm all in."

"Come with me," my father said, putting his hand on Dean's shoulder. "Let's go serve some justice."

I smiled, gave the two most important men in my life hugs, then watched them as they entered the judge's back room. About ten minutes later, they both emerged with giant smiles across their faces.

The judge appeared minutes later. After ordering for everyone to be seated, he put on his reading glasses and read from a folder.

"Based off evidence provided and accusations, this trial will be closed. Mr Blake Salato will no longer be charged for assault, battery, harassment, and attempted sexual assault. The case against Mr Salato will be re-opened with plaintiff Dean Marks in regards to his brother Alexander Marks. Mr Salato will be charged with second-degree murder. Until the hearing, Mr Salato will be detained in our juvenile correctional facility."

With great uproar, the court room burst with excitement. Everyone was wildly baffled as they loudly discussed the news. Murder? They all exclaimed to each other, shocked to hear the turn of events. The news had been dropped like a bomb, exploding with a fierce rupture. Nobody could have predicted it; it came straight out of left field.

The attorney called "objection!" and protested over the noise but there was no use. Out of the corner of my eye, I could see Blake bury his face into his hands. I hadn't quite won yet, but seeing the look on Blake's father's face as he was carried away in handcuffs was satisfaction enough. But I knew, deep down in my heart, that there was no way we could lose.

Good always wins.

My journey was over, but Blake's was just beginning. His future was now dark and bleak, like his heart. I had zero sympathy in destroying his life. After all, he destroyed not only mine; but my fathers, my boyfriend, and my boyfriend's brother. He wasn't going to see the outside world for a very long time, and he had gotten nothing less than what he deserved.

EPILOGUE

1 8 Months Later

For once, I could finally say that my life was relatively normal. Once Blake was out of the picture, everything in my life fell into place.

My father, Dean, and Blake all went to trial six months later. It was weird being un-involved and on the other side for once. But I helped out as much as I could. Both of them worked long and hard, and did whatever it took to make sure that Alex Marks did not die in vain. An innocent life was lost, but a guilty man would be punished.

After a month long trial, Blake Salato was officially charged with second-degree murder and order at least twenty five years in prison.

God only knows where he is now. I only hope that wherever he is, he drops the soap in the shower.

My mother eventually accepted reality, accepted that Dean was a much better guy than Blake was, and most of all, accepted me. My brother not only forgot about Blake, but also considers Dean as his idol now. My father received so much publicity and recognition from winning the case that he was able to open his own law firm.

As for Dean . . . his life took a similar turn down the right path. After his brother died, the Black Knights officially broke up, allowing Dean to leave that part of his tainted past behind and focus on his future.

Together, we survived the rest of high school, and encountered only the kind of problems that average teenagers faced. Lucy forgave me after I told her everything. Of course, she was mad for hiding so much from her but ultimately she understood. Through-out senior year, we even went on a few double dates.

As I slowly reminisced about my high school years -- the good and the bad -- I tapped my pencil and miserably tried to capture the essence of my experiences into words. After all, I had been a lot. How could a mere 500-word speech communicate all of that without droning on or sharing too much? The task seemed impossible. But as I had proven last year, nothing was impossible.

This is it, Riley, the voice in my head encouraged. The moment you've waited years for. Your time to shine.

"And now, a word from our valedictorian," Principal Werner announced. "Riley Jennings."

A roar of applause from the audience filled with family members filled my ears as I wobbled to my feet. I felt a bead of sweat form at my forehead as I approached the podium; I had never been very good at public speaking, and the gown I was wearing was unbearably hot.

"Hi everyone," I muttered into the microphone, hearing my voice echo through the gym. "Thank you all for coming . . ." I paused, looking over at my fellow classmates in their seats, scan-ning for Dean's warm face.

When I found him smiling up at me, I continued. "The past four years I have spent here at Oxford High have been . . . interesting. You could say there was never a dull moment, and I think everyone in my class can say the same. High school has not just been a place of learning, but a place of adventure and growth. I know that I am not the same person I was when back when I was freshmen.

Here, we have learned about inverse functions and quantum theories, things that don't really matter. But we have also learned about things that do matter, like individuality and strength. I can say that I graduate prepared for the real word, prepared to face real world problems, and prepared to face all odds. I can say that I leave Oxford High, grateful for what it has done for me. I am proud to say that I'm ready to take the next step in my life, head on, without fear. I can overcome anything that comes my way . . . just like all of you can."

The echo of my last words was muffled out by the applause and cheers it had caused. I went back to my seat and beamed with satisfaction. Not much long after, my graduating class took that ceremonial walk, gathered our well-earned diplomas, threw our caps in the air, and celebrated.

I made the rounds, starting with my parents and working my way back. I was stopped along the way to be congratulated and praised. I thanked them each time, then pushed my way on, finally reaching my destination. Dean threw his arms around me and lifted me off the ground. I kissed him deeply, and never felt so happy. His mother came over to us, and sent her regards.

"My baby boy is all grown up," she teased, pinching her son's cheek. "Attending Berklee College of Music and everything. I'm so proud," she exclaimed with a bright tone, ignoring the fact that she had tears in her eyes. "Take care of him."

"I will," I replied, chuckling lightly. I felt equally as proud as she did. I watched as this slacker who was deemed to go nowhere turned his life around, worked his butt off, and followed his passion.

"Dean said you'd be in Boston with him, but he didn't tell me where you were going," she said, nudging Dean in the arm. "Let me guess . . . Harvard?"

I shook my head, and resisted the urge to roll my eyes. If I had a nickel for every time somebody made that assumption, I'd have enough to pay for my college tuition.

"Boston College . . . not Ivy League, but just as good," I announced, proud at that very fact alone.

I had defied the expectations everyone had for me, done it my way, and everything turned out just fine The same applied to Dean as well. Before, we both suffered from the same unfortunate, miserable destiny. The strength to change that destiny always rested inside of us, but we needed each other to release our inner fortitude.

The power of love and support can do extraordinary things, bring out the best and worst in us, release our inner thoughts and dreams, and most of all, beat all odds. You can't fight love once it's been found, you can't hold back when your only option is to move forward, you can't make changes if you don't take risks, and you can't live life with a moment of regret.

I learned this the hard way, I learned this through trial and error. I learned this because a strange, mysterious boy waltzed into my life, gave me hope and gave me strength, and changed my life forever.

www.ingramcontent.com/pod-product-compliance
Lightning Source LLC
Chambersburg PA
CBHW070935190726
48292CB00004B/1194